Birrung
the
Secret
Friend

Birrung
the
Secret
Friend

JACKIE FRENCH

Angus&Robertson
An imprint of HarperCollins*Children's Books*

Angus&Robertson
An imprint of HarperCollins*Children'sBooks*, Australia

First published in Australia in 2015
by HarperCollins*Publishers* Australia Pty Limited
ABN 36 009 913 517
harpercollins.com.au

Text copyright © Jackie French 2015
Illustrations copyright © Mark Wilson 2015

HarperCollins*Publishers*
Level 13, 201 Elizabeth Street, Sydney NSW 2000, Australia
Unit D1, 63 Apollo Drive, Rosedale, Auckland 0632, New Zealand
A 53, Sector 57, Noida, UP, India
77–85 Fulham Palace Road, London W6 8JB, United Kingdom
2 Bloor Street East, 20th floor, Toronto, Ontario M4W 1A8, Canada
195 Broadway, New York NY 10007, USA

National Library of Australia Cataloguing-in-Publication data:

French, Jackie, author.
   Birrung the secret friend / Jackie French.
   ISBN: 978 0 7322 9943 9 (paperback)
   ISBN: 978 1 4607 0321 2 (ebook)
   For ages 7–10.
   Secret friends—Juvenile fiction.
A823.3

Cover design by HarperCollins Design Studio
Cover illustration by Mark Wilson
Cover images: Girl by Penny Tweedie / Alamy; background textures by
shutterstock.com
Author photograph by Kelly Sturgiss
Typeset in Berkeley Old Style Book by Kirby Jones
Printed and bound in Australia by Griffin Press
The papers used by HarperCollins in the manufacture of this book are a natural,
recyclable product made from wood grown in sustainable plantation forests.
The fibre source and manufacturing processes meet recognised international
environmental standards, and carry certification.

To Colin Mackellar,
first chaplain to the moon
and much loved successor to
Mr Johnson, with gratitude

CHAPTER 1

Cheese

Sydney Cove, December 1789

I waited in the line outside the storehouse. Only two convicts were before me — big fellows with tattoos on their arms and dirty bare feet — waiting for their rations too. My tummy was so empty it couldn't even gurgle.

There was cheese in that storehouse.

I wanted that cheese so bad I could already feel the maggots wriggling against my tongue. Ma used to say that maggots meant food was going bad, but when your tummy is empty, maggots are just extra food. I'd been eating maggots with my cheese for the two years we'd

1

been here in New South Wales, and hadn't even got a tummy ache. Not from the maggots, anyways. Hunger ached worse than bad food.

Elsie and me hadn't eaten for all yesterday. The storehouse only gave out the rations on Saturdays and Wednesdays. I snuck out to get mine as soon as it got light and the drum went *rat-a-tat-tat* to call the convicts to work. The convicts in this line must be too sick to work. I hoped they didn't have the strength to grab my rations before I could get them back to Elsie. But they looked big.

Just about everyone in the colony was bigger than me. I was small, even for a ten-year-old. How can you grow tall on the slops fed to you in an English gaol or down in the dark and wet hold of a convict ship?

The man in front of me had his arm in a sling, but he looked as strong as a bullock. I wasn't going to let him take my cheese. And nothing else neither.

Elsie didn't get no rations, so we had to live on mine. We didn't have no way to keep them safe: ants or rats could eat them, or some thief nick them. So we ate our food as soon as we got it, even if we went hungry in between.

Only Bullock Man in front of me now. He was nearly as tall as the wild Indians who lived around the colony,

2

but soft looking, not muscled like them, from being chained for nearly a year down in the ships that brought us here, and probably from doing as little as he could since our arrival. Ma used to say most convicts were so lazy they'd eat their toe nails — or someone else's — before bothering to open an oyster.

Bullock Man peered in the storehouse door. The storehouse was made of mud, like almost every building in the colony, with big holes from rain and rats. If them holes get any bigger, I thought, those walls won't keep out robbers, not in a colony of thieves. They'd get our cheese — and all the other food too.

Food! I was nearly there. My tummy did rumble now.

The storeman measured Bullock Man's rations into his pannikin: three cups of flour, a lump of salt pork, rice. The storeman was a convict, like Ma had been. I was no convict. I'd been born free, even if I'd had to stay most of my life with Ma in Newgate Prison back in England, and come with her on the ship here.

Bullock Man stared at the rice and flour and salt pork in his pannikin. 'Where's me cheese?'

'All gone,' said the storeman.

'Gone?' demanded Bullock Man. My heart sank as low as my empty tummy. Rice and flour had to be cooked! But me and Elsie could have eaten that cheese straight away.

The storeman winked at me. 'You got rice instead,' he told Bullock Man. 'Make yourself a nice pudding.'

'What with?' Bullock Man demanded. He had a point. The governor and some of the officers had cows or goats with milk to make a rice pudding. Not the likes of me or Bullock Man.

Bullock Man bent down till his head was at the same height as the storeman's. He grinned, showing two black teeth and swollen red gums. 'You give me that cheese or somefink nasty is going to happen to you one o' these nights.'

The storeman grinned back. He had four teeth, long yellow ones. 'You might have been a high and mighty back home in Todger's Lane, matey, with your thief chums bashing folks over their heads to get their purses. But I'm boss of this storehouse. Off with you! Or you'll find I've run out of salt pork too on Saturdays.'

'You ain't no better than me! You was a pickpocket! At least I had me cudgels. Better than a sneak thief.'

The storeman stopped grinning. 'This is a new land, matey. I got a responsible job. I'm king of the storehouse here. So hop it.'

Bullock Man didn't hop. But he did move away, muttering, to the corner of the storehouse. He pretended he was leaning on the building to rub his ankle. I moved up to the storeman, keeping a close watch on Bullock Man out of the corner of my eye.

The storeman grinned at me. 'Well, Barney Bean, you been growing like a good little bean?'

I worked up a smile for him. You try living with a name like 'Bean'. 'Very funny, sir.'

'You still ain't got no pannikin?'

I shrugged. Some thieving Johnny had stolen my pannikin the night Ma died, and there weren't no more left in the stores to give out. Wasn't much of anything in the colony any more, except rags and lags and mud. Even most of the Indians had vanished since their plague. We'd been at Port Jackson for nearly two years now, and there'd been no store ship to bring us food and new clothes or spades or pannikins or even news. England and the whole world over the horizon could have vanished and we'd never know.

You can't boil dried peas or rice without a pannikin. That's why me and Elsie needed cheese. You don't need to cook cheese. And the storeman knew it. I held out my sheet of bark.

'Fish or salt pork?' asked the storeman.

I hesitated. You got more fish than pork. But fish goes bad quick.

'Pork,' I said reluctantly.

The storeman measured out my salt pork. I only got two-thirds of what a grown-up got. The pork was a square as big as my thumb, hard as a brick and dark as coal. It tasted like coal too. It took a lot of chewing, but didn't need cooking either.

Next he measured out my flour. It smelled a bit and wriggled with weevils, but they were no more trouble to me than the maggots. Elsie and me could mix that into damper with water from the Tank Stream and cook it in the ashes of someone else's fire — after everyone had gone to sleep, of course, so no one could pinch it.

It was too dangerous to try to keep our own fire going, even if we was cold, in case more thugs found us. Me and Elsie hadn't anything left to steal, except our clothes and a bit of food, but I was afraid that someone might hurt Elsie. Even if they didn't, a stranger would scare her bad. I reckoned Elsie had been scared enough already.

The storeman winked at me again. He held a tiny hunk of cheese, down low where no one could see it.

I could have eaten that cheese in one gulp. I reached

out to take it quickly, afore Bullock Man could see it. My hand trembled with hunger.

The cheese dropped to the ground. I grabbed it, brushing off the dirt.

I glanced around. Had Bullock Man seen?

He had. He stared at my cheese, like it was all the jewels of China. Then he looked at me. His grin spread right across his face, like butter melting.

Even a maggot would guess that Bullock Man planned to grab my rations as soon as I walked past him. But he couldn't attack me while the storeman was watching. The storeman really was a king, here at the end of the world.

Someone else watched me too — a girl walking down the muddy track. She was an Indian, one of the natives with black skin. There'd been hundreds of them around when our ships first got here, so many canoes on the harbour with the women fishing and cooking on their smoky fires right there on the water, and feeding fish to their kids.

The whole harbour had smelled of cooking fish. Sometimes I'd wished I was an Indian, so I could fill my belly with fish too. But back then I had Ma, who was the best ma in the world, even if she wasn't much good as a pickpocket. And then the Indians vanished, except the dead bodies along the beaches. We'd waited for the plague to kill us too. But it hadn't. Just the Indians, lying dead on the beaches all around the harbour.

But here was an Indian again! A live one! She was clothed properly in a dress and shoes. A clean dress, all bright with tiny blue flowers on it, not the nothing colour of convicts' clothes.

She was tall, with lots of black hair all shiny in a halo about her head. She was the most beautiful girl I had seen in my life, even with the black skin and all. To be fair I hadn't seen many pretty girls. It was hard for a girl to look pretty in Newgate, or on the ships that brought us here, down in the dark in the water with dead rats and other stuff I didn't want to think about all rolling around us on our bunks.

There weren't many girls in the colony at all. Governor Phillip had sent most of the young'uns to Norfolk Island, to keep them safe from the convict men. In fact the only girl I knew at all was Elsie, and she was a skinned mouse.

The Indian girl smiled at me as she passed. She was fifteen, maybe. Her teeth were strong and white. Couldn't remember ever seeing teeth as strong and white as hers. Couldn't remember when I'd last seen a smile either.

Suddenly I forgot how much my tummy hurt with hunger, how the huts around me were crumbling from the rain. The blue sky seemed to dance above the harbour. For a breath or two everything was beautiful, the pale blue new leaves on the native trees, a flock of birds, red and green, yelling above us. I wondered if this girl knew how to sail a canoe, and catch fish, and cook it ...

My tummy clenched. I shouldn't have thought about cooked fish.

When the plague back in autumn had killed just about every Indian in the world, Surgeon White managed to save two of them, a boy and a girl. Surgeon White had adopted the boy. This must be the black girl Ma told me the clergyman Mr Johnson and his wife were looking after. When we first came here, Ma'd said the Indians might all creep into the colony and at night murder us in our beds. But it'd been them that died.

I'd glimpsed the Indian girl far off, in her fine clothes, walking with Mr Johnson. But I'd never seen her close like this before, so tall and straight. Her smile was as bright as the sunlight after rain.

But I didn't have time to think about smiles and pretty girls. I had to get this food back safe to Elsie. And I had to eat something soon, or I'd go all wobbly and fall faint in the muck on the road and some cove would steal my clothes too, and leave me with nothing except my teeth and some of the coves here would steal those too.

I began to trudge back along the track between the huts, my feet squishing in the mud from last night's storm. Most of the walls were half washed away already, and the cabbage-tree-frond roofs were rotting.

Bullock Man followed me. Just like I knew he would.

I'd be safe while the storeman could see me. But I had to turn the corner soon. I knew some tricks that would protect me against coves like this. I'd bitten a man's leg once when he tried to steal my damper, and poured a shovel full of coals on a man's head when he grabbed Ma, while Ma was already busy kneeing him in the stomach and squashing his nose with her fist. But this time I was on my own. If I bit Bullock Man, I might startle him enough to let go of me long enough to escape. But I'd have lost my rations.

I'd have to run as soon as I got to the corner. Fast!

One! Two! Three! I began to sprint, fast as a rabbit, except there weren't any in New South Wales. Fast as a lizard, maybe.

I heard Bullock Man's feet pound behind me. He was big, but he was fast too. He was nearly onto me! I could smell him, sweat and dirt and rotting teeth. I heard him laugh. And then I heard …

'*Ow!*'

I glanced back. Bullock Man grabbed his knee in agony. He stared at a rock at his feet.

Had someone thrown that rock at him?

No time to find out. I ran.

CHAPTER 2

Me and Elsie

I ran past the huts, all higgledy-piggledy along the shore, then climbed the hill between the cliffs streaked with seagull droppings and onto the beach. You could see the harbour from here, blue and grey, with its green fingers covered in trees. It was empty now, of course, apart from its tiny islands, with no Indian canoes or the big transport ships that had brought us from England. I couldn't even see the colony's own two tiny ships. They'd sailed off somewhere. England? Norfolk Island? To get more food? No one told the likes of me.

We were stranded here, hungry and ragged. Except I'd been hungry and ragged back in England too. At least here I had the harbour and the bright birds — Ma had loved those birds — and no rats trying to bite my face like there'd been back in prison.

Now I had Elsie too. And today we weren't even going to be hungry!

I stopped for breath, enjoying the harbour and the tickle of the breeze, then ran down into the colony's huts again. That was the trick, see? No place to hide in the bush. Even the trees had tall straight trunks you couldn't climb unless you were an Indian. But in the straggle of huts up from the beach there was this one shack that had half fallen down. If you pulled a bit of roof aside and squeezed underneath, there was a tiny room, big enough for me and Elsie to sit up or lie down in.

It wasn't much. But it was safe. It even kept most of the rain off us. I'd pinched another blanket. I'd pulled up grass and bracken to make a bed too, just like Ma had shown me.

Elsie stared up at me as I slipped under the roof then carefully pulled it over us, her face small and white in the dimness. She got scared being alone. I grinned and held out the cheese. 'Got it!' I whispered.

Elsie didn't say anything. Elsie never said anything. Elsie couldn't talk. Don't know why. She'd never said a word since I'd found her. Never smiled neither. But she almost smiled then. She gazed at that cheese like it was a chest of treasure.

I'd have hugged her, but Elsie didn't like being touched, except when we huddled up for warmth at night. I crouched next to her and broke the cheese in half.

'Don't eat it too fast,' I reminded her. Ma taught me that. If you eat too fast when you're hungry, you vomit it up and then you're worse off than before.

I took a nibble of cheese. Oh, it was good. I nibbled again. I tried not to think of the first months in the colony when Ma was alive. I was never hungry then. I had a tent to sleep in, and fire outside, as big as we wanted because the trees here dropped so much dead wood it looked like they grew it just for folks like us to burn.

The third day after we landed at Sydney Cove was the first time I had enough to eat in my life. Two days of stumbling, feeling the land go up and down like the sea, while all the sheep and cows and pigs stumbled around us. I'd have laughed if I hadn't felt so dizzy. Then the governor ordered Ma and some other women to gather oysters, down on the harbour rocks … and me too.

Oh, them oysters. Small and sweet and tasting of the sea. I just sat and ate and ate till no more would fit in my stomach while Ma and the others bashed them with rocks, then put the shells in big bags to burn to make the stuff called lime that held the bricks together that were used to build the officers' chimneys and the governor's house.

Day after day we ate those oysters. Most of the women were assigned to care for the officers, but not Ma and the other oyster-shell gatherers. I grew so fast my trousers almost rode up to my knees. I didn't care. Ma and I were warm and safe and our bellies were full. After the work bell rang each afternoon Ma and I could do what we wanted, gather wood for the fire, or more bracken for our beds. Every night we sat by the fire and Ma made damper in the ashes — someone called it that because the coals had to be damped down so the outside didn't burn and waste precious flour — and a stew of peas and salt pork and watercress picked from the stream in our pannikins. Ma held me close and sang me songs, songs I'd never heard before because she'd always been too tired, her belly too empty to have energy for singing.

We'd had a year here, me and Ma. And then Ma died.

I ate my last crumb of cheese slowly. I'd sleep with the rest of the rations under my shirt tonight, to keep them from the rats and ants. 'We can eat the pork tomorrow morning,' I told Elsie. 'Then tomorrow night I'll find a fire to cook some damper.'

Elsie looked scared again. Scared someone might find her when I wasn't there. Scared I might not come back too. It was dangerous going out after dark. Some of the convicts had been made nightwatchmen: they bashed you up good if they found you out at night. But I was good at keeping to the shadows. And flour made you sick if you ate it raw. I knew. I'd tried.

'Maybe even find some oysters if I can sneak around to a cove where no one will see me,' I added. Oysters were free for the gathering, but if the convict foremen saw, they'd put me to work. If I had to work, Elsie'd be alone all day. I patted her hand. She didn't draw it back any more. She knew I wouldn't hurt her. 'Don't worry. I won't get caught. I'm the best hider in the colony!' I boasted. 'No one can ever find me! I'm —'

I stopped. I heard voices not far away. Footsteps coming closer. Elsie froze. Had Bullock Man found us?

I clenched my fists. No one was going to hurt Elsie without a fight.

Someone scrabbled at the ruins of the hut. I'd been followed all right.

'There he is!' The hut roof lifted off us. Light speared into the hut, so bright I couldn't see who was out there.

Elsie rolled quickly under a bit of fallen roof, silent as a mouse, invisible. She couldn't talk, but she could hear danger good enough.

I hoped whoever was out there hadn't seen her hide. No use trying to run, not trapped among the wreckage of the hut. I was cornered. I blinked up at the light.

'You can have me rations. Here.' I held them out. Just don't hit me, I thought. If you hurt me too bad, I can't bring Elsie water. We can live for a few days more with no food, but we can't live without water. Please, don't find Elsie …

'I don't want your rations, boy.' I looked up, my eyes still getting used to the light. It wasn't Bullock Man. This man sounded like a gentleman. He even sounded gentle too. 'Come out of there.' He also sounded like he was used to telling people what to do.

I glanced back into the shadows of the fallen hut. Elsie was still hidden. I wriggled out into the daylight and stood up.

And there was the black girl, just like she'd looked by the storehouse, except now she wore a bonnet over her hair. She grinned at me, triumphant because she'd tracked me down, showing those white teeth again.

I glanced at the man she was with, ready to hand over the food fast, so he'd go away. Then I relaxed a bit. He was only Mr Johnson, the chaplain to the colony. We were all supposed to go to church to listen to him preach each Sunday, except there wasn't a church, just a big tree Mr Johnson stood under, or a crumbling storeroom when it rained. Most of the convicts didn't bother to go, and no one made them either. Neither Elsie nor I went, of course, because Elsie was scared and I couldn't leave her. But when Ma was alive, I'd liked the singing, and how Mr Johnson spoke to us like we were people just like him, not convict scum. Not that I was a convict, but you know what I mean.

And here was Mr Johnson now, not in his good Sunday suit, but the old rusty black he wore when he was in his garden. Mr Johnson had the biggest vegetable garden in the colony. Three big plots, one near his house and another two Ma had told me that he'd bought from one of the soldiers.

Mr Johnson would want my weevily flour, or salt pork. I bobbed my head to him politely, like Ma had shown me. 'Sir,' I said.

Mr Johnson lifted his hat to me, just like I was a gentleman. I'd have lifted my cap for him, except I'd lost the cap I'd been given on the ship or, most likely, someone had nicked it.

'Good morning,' said Mr Johnson, just like I was a blooming duke. 'I am Mr Johnson and this is Abaroo, a member of our family.'

'Hello,' said the black girl.

My jaw dropped. I hadn't known Indians spoke proper words. I shut my mouth before the flies could land in it. Then I said, 'My name's Barney Bean. I weren't doing nothing wrong, sir.'

'I wasn't doing anything wrong,' he corrected. 'No one is accusing you of wrongdoing, lad. But perhaps wrong has been done *to* you.'

He looked at our hut. My cheeks grew hot. Our hut stank. There wasn't much I could do about that. It was filthy too, and so was I.

'Where's your mother?' Mr Johnson didn't ask where my pa was, like someone might in England. Almost no young'un in the colony had a pa, not one who'd claim them, anyhow.

'Ma is dead, sir. My pa died when I were a baby,' I added.

19

His voice was even gentler. 'I'm sorry, lad. How did your mother die?'

'Cut on her hand from an oyster shell. It puffed up red and then she died. Mr White did his best.' Mr White had been good to Ma. He'd even made the hospital convicts give me dinner while I sat with Ma before she died.

'No one looks after you?'

'I looks after me!'

Mr Johnson looked at the rotting hut I'd crawled out of. Then he looked at me. I squirmed, embarrassed at how dirty I was. Even in prison and on the ship Ma had taught me to try to keep my face clean. At last he seemed to reach a decision. 'How would you like a job?'

I glowered at him. 'Don't have to do no job. I ain't no convict.'

'We are all born into this world to work,' said Mr Johnson. He held out his hands. They had calluses and cracked nails. All the officers' hands here were soft, like a gentleman's. 'We should labour for each other according to the will of God. If you work for me, you will have a room to sleep in. Not much of a room,' he added. 'But better than this. You will eat at my table. The food is simple, but there is plenty of it.' He smiled. 'I believe I have the biggest potatoes in all of the colony.'

Potatoes! I hadn't eaten a potato since before we left England. There'd been a hot potato seller on the street as Ma was led in chains to the cart to take us to the ship. She used her last farthing to buy me one. I'd held that potato till it was almost cold, loving its warmth.

'How many potatoes?' I asked. I wasn't going to work for one potato a day, no matter how big it was.

'All you want to eat,' said Mr Johnson calmly. 'If you dig my garden well and help me weed it. And follow the rules of our home.'

I looked at him suspiciously. 'What are they?'

'No swearing. No insolence to me or my wife. To treat each other as you'd like to be treated.'

I could do all that, I reckoned. To work in a garden! I loved watching the gardens grow in the colony. Nothing but tussocks and trees when we'd landed, two years back, then bare dirt. But then people put in seeds and soon there'd been bits of green, then big plants growing. I'd watched a man pull a carrot out of the ground and eat it. It was like magic — food coming out of the dirt. Lot of the plants had died. But not Mr Johnson's.

Mr Johnson would let me work in his garden! Feed me potatoes. He'd teach me the magic that made his garden give so much food. Maybe one day I'd even get land for a garden of me own …

But I couldn't do it. I had to keep Elsie safe. She wasn't strong enough to work. Even if Mr Johnson would take a girl who couldn't speak, Elsie would be too scared to go with him.

'No,' I said. Then added, 'Thank you, sir,' as Ma would have wanted me to.

Mr Johnson stared at me. 'Lad, I'm offering you a second chance. You don't have to live like this.'

We'll have a second chance at Botany Bay, Ma had said to me as we sat in the ship in the stink below deck.

And now I couldn't take it.

'No, sir. Thank you, sir,' I said again.

Mr Johnson shrugged. 'Very well.' He turned away. It was like the sun had slid down behind the mountain, but this time it would never come up again! I'd lost my chance. But I'd done the right thing …

'Mr-Johnson-sir.' The black girl made it sound like one word.

He looked back at us. Abaroo lifted the bit of roof. Elsie stared up at us, white as a rabbit, her arms around her legs and body as if she was trying to make herself so small they couldn't see her.

'Ah.' Mr Johnson bent down. He didn't touch her. He smiled, the gentlest smile I'd ever seen. 'What's your name, child?'

'Her name's Elsie.'

'Let her speak for herself, lad,' he said quietly.

'She can't talk. She's dumb. Not stupid,' I said quickly. 'Just can't say anything.'

'She is your sister? Has she always been like this?'

'She's my sister now.' I'd found Elsie the day after Ma died. She'd been curled up under one of the rock ledges, trying to make herself tiny like she was now. Looked like she hadn't eaten for days, or hardly ever. 'Don't know where she came from. Don't know why she can't talk neither. I call her Elsie 'cause it was me ma's name. That's all I can tell you, sir.'

And it was the truth. I'd thought and thought about where Elsie mighta come from. But I couldn't find no answer. And Elsie couldn't tell me neither.

It was a mystery, like how the moon knew how to follow the same path across the sky each night. There weren't a lot of us in the colony — few enough to know everyone pretty much by sight. I'd have seen another young'un in the colony, especially since most got sent away.

Where had Elsie come from? How had she got under that rock? And why couldn't she speak? I knew she had a tongue, because I saw it when she ate.

Mr Johnson looked at me as though I'd done something great, like Captain Cook finding this place or King Someone Or Other winning a war with France. 'You look after a stranger? That's a true Christian thing to do, my boy.'

I shrugged. I didn't want to say it had been cold, sleeping by myself. At first Elsie was just someone to huddle with at night. But then, well, I don't know. She needed me. It felt good to be needed, like I wasn't just a worthless urchin. And there was something about her that was, well, Elsie, that made me want to look after her.

'Is she why you won't come and work for me?'

I nodded. 'Elsie gets scared, see? Scared if there's strange men about. Too scared to get rations or even water. Won't even let me touch her, except pat her on the hand ...'

Abaroo knelt next to Elsie. She touched her cheek with one black hand.

Elsie didn't pull away.

I stared. 'She never let me do that ...'

Beside us, Abaroo helped Elsie to her feet. Elsie weren't too steady — she'd never walked much all the time I'd known her, hiding away. Abaroo put her arm around her, to help her walk.

And Elsie let her.

I stared at Abaroo. She wasn't just the most beautiful girl I had ever seen. She was like one of the angels Mr Johnson talked about in a sermon when Ma was alive. Abaroo had saved me from Bullock Man. Now she was leading me — and leading Elsie too — towards the new life Mr Johnson had promised us.

'One day,' said Mr Johnson quietly, 'there will be a refuge in this colony for all orphans. There will be food for body and mind and soul for every child who needs it. Until then, will you come with me?'

I didn't have to answer. Abaroo was leading Elsie along the muddy track. Mr Johnson and I followed her.

CHAPTER 3

House and Garden

'Wash,' said Sally.

Sally was Mr and Mrs Johnson's servant.

She was as skinny as a ferret and had two hairs on her chin. She hadn't seemed too happy to see Mr Johnson bring two filthy children into their clean house. But Mrs Johnson had smiled at us like he'd brought her the king's crown, not two grubby brats.

Now Sally pointed to the water trough behind the shed. Mr Johnson had a proper well with planks around it so no one would fall in. Most other people washed in the Tank Stream, and got their water from it too. It was pretty when I first saw it, with ferns and flowers. It was stinking mud now.

Sally glared at me like I was something a dog had dropped. 'You wash every bit of your body, then draw up fresh water and wash your clothes. You wash them till they don't smell at all. When they're dry and you're clean and dressed, you can come inside. And if I can smell anything but soap and water, you're going back outside.'

I didn't like Sally ordering me about. She was a convict and I was free. But I had a feeling Sally was the one who cooked the potatoes.

What was soap? I hoped that was good to eat too.

'What's happening to Elsie?'

'The mistress and that Abaroo are washing her inside.' Sally handed me a bowl of goo.

'What's that?'

'Soap. You never used soap before?' Sally sighed. 'You rub it on yourself, then wash it off. Makes the dirt come off. Rub it into your clothes too, then rinse them. Pour the water onto the garden.'

I sniffed it. 'What's it made of?'

'Lard and wood ash … Look, never you mind what it's made of. You just use it.'

Soap was funny stuff, all right. Made me skin all slippery and covered with bubbles. I had to haul up bucket after bucket of water to get it off me. But, like Sally said, it got the dirt off. It tasted terrible though, when I ate a bit, even worse than the butter they'd given us in the rations, till it ran out.

I sat in the sun, leaning against the shed till my clothes dried, listening to the noises, leaves rustling and birds' wings up above and things going *creak*, *creak*, *creak* in the grass. I'd grown up with noise in the prison and on the ship, but that was people noise, except for the wind and sea. I'd never heard land noise till I come here.

I could see the garden from here. Big plants and little plants and tiny plants in bare ground. I wondered which ones grew the potatoes. Did you pick potatoes off trees like apples and acorns? Two convict men dug the tussocks with mattocks, but slowly, like they'd been dipped in treacle.

One day, I thought, I'll have a hundred potato trees of my own.

I peered around the shed at the house. It was made of cabbage-tree logs stuck together with mud with a bark roof, like all the houses except the governor's, but bigger and better made than most. The walls sagged a bit, but someone had propped them up with poles. It had a proper stone chimney, with smoke coming out of it, and two lean-to rooms out the back, where logs had been propped against the wall and covered with sheets of bark, with a rough wooden door at one end. And all around was even more garden, full of all kinds of plants, ones that grew up and ones that climbed over the ground.

Down past the garden was the big pit, with ragged convicts digging clay to make bricks — or digging when the overseer was watching, and sitting down when he wasn't. Beyond the pit was the bush. Then more bush, and more, until the mountains rose up, dark blue against the clear blue sky.

'You, boy! You coming in for your dinner?' That was Sally, her voice as sharp as a pickpocket's knife.

I scrambled into my clothes, even though they were still damp, and ran through the door, then slowed down and looked around again.

I'd never seen a room like this one, not in prison or before. It was … clean, even with its mud walls and dirt floor. The floor was packed down hard and all the loose dirt had been swept away. The walls looked like they'd been swept too. And it was more than clean. There was a sort of quiet. It was pretty too. I had never thought a room could be pretty.

A table in the middle had a flowered cloth spread over it — all that cloth just on a table. And plates on it, shiny white china ones like I'd seen in shops, not battered tin or even pewter. And books, right up one wall, like Mr Johnson's house was a book shop, and more plates on shelves along another wall, like they were in a shop too. And a big hearth made of flat stones fitted together next to the fireplace with its wood fire, and a big pot hanging over it out of which came a smell that was better than anything I'd ever known.

I forced my eyes away from the pot. Mr Johnson sat at the table with the Indian girl and Mrs Johnson. Mrs Johnson was pretty too in a shawl and green dress. Beside her sat Elsie, in a blue dress that was too big for her, but sort of bundled up at the waist with a scarf for a belt so it didn't drag on the ground. Her hair was clean like mine. She looked scared, but not like she was going to run.

Then I looked at the pot.

Mrs Johnson smiled at me. She had all her teeth, it looked like. I'd never known a woman her age who had all her teeth like that. 'Sit down, Barney. Welcome to our poor home.'

It didn't look poor to me. I sat next to Abaroo. She grinned at me.

Mr Johnson bent his head. He shut his eyes. So did Mrs Johnson and Abaroo. Sally gave me a cuff on the ear. 'Shut your eyes while the master says grace,' she hissed.

'Who's Grace?'

Mr Johnson opened his eyes. 'Grace is when we give thanks to God for the treasures he has given us.'

If treasures meant the food in that pot, I would say 'thanks' all right. So I shut my eyes and waited till Mr Johnson's voice had stopped.

Then I looked at the food.

CHAPTER 4

Dinner

Food!

You should have seen what came out of that pot. First of all Sally lifted out a pease pudding, wrapped in a white cloth, with a pair of tongs. She undid the cloth and cut off a great slice for each of us and put them on our plates. It had bits of meat in it — real fresh meat, not salt pork. Then four fat boiled potatoes on every plate, a pile of boiled cabbage, a smaller pile of sliced boiled carrots, and a red boiled vegetable I'd never seen before. I tried to eat with a knife and fork, but it was too slow. That food smelled so good and I was so hungry. I picked up a slab of pudding in my fingers and shoved it in my mouth, then looked around to see if anyone minded.

Mr and Mrs Johnson pretended not to notice.

I stared. My mouth fell open, still full of pudding. There was Elsie on the other side of the table, using her knife and fork, one in each hand, like she had used them all her life.

Then Sally sat down next to Elsie. A servant and convict eating at a gentleman's table, instead of eating in the kitchen — if there'd been a kitchen, which there wasn't, or at least out on the back step, though there wasn't actually a step either.

But it was no stranger than a black girl and the two of us eating with a lady and gentleman. Sally even knew how to use a knife and fork, and so did Abaroo. I was going to have to learn to use them fast.

Mrs Johnson neatly forked up a piece of carrot, chewed and swallowed. I tried to copy how she did it. 'What did you see down at the harbour, Abaroo?' she asked. I glanced at Mrs Johnson's belly under her shawl, then looked away before Sally saw me noticing. I reckoned Mrs Johnson was going to have a baby one day.

Abaroo considered. 'Men.'

Men down at the harbour? Well, we weren't going to stand up and cheer about that news, were we? Not like maybe a ship at last from England, or the Frenchies attacking. I got on with eating. One potato, two potatoes, more of that good pease pudding.

The drum rolled down at the barracks, the signal it was time convicts could stop work. You could hear it even up here.

The back door opened. The two convicts came in from the garden and sat at the table too. Sally got up and gave them dinner. The men didn't talk much, just shovelled food in, like me.

'More potatoes?' asked Sally.

More? I had three helpings of them potatoes, eight big fat ones, and some more of the boiled red things. I was as full as I'd ever been in my life. It was a better sort of being full than a tummy of oysters too.

Then Sally pulled out another big round cloth from the pot, and inside it was a plum pudding. It was the first time I'd met one of those, but me and that pudding became good friends fast. I didn't even feel sick from eating so much.

The convict men went back to their own hut then, as it was after work hours for convicts. They said they had their own garden to work in there, though I reckoned coves like them would just put their feet up. If there'd been a pub, they'd have gone there, but one of the things the colony didn't have much of any more was beer or porter, so there weren't pubs neither.

I pushed my chair back from the table. 'What happens now?' I asked.

What happened then was that Sally showed me where Elsie would sleep, with her in one of the lean-to rooms out the back. I would sleep in the other, with the big sacks of potatoes and strings of onions and a crock of goat's cheese. I imagined sleeping with all that food around me. I reckoned I'd have the best dreams in the world.

Mr Johnson made me what he called a camp bed, lengths of wood with cloth strung between them. Whoever heard of a gentleman making furniture like a carpenter? Mr Johnson grinned when I said that, as though I'd said something funny.

Elsie had a proper bed that had been used by the Johnsons' servant Elizabeth. But Sally said she'd been whipped for insolence and sent to Norfolk Island. I wasn't sure what 'insolence' was exactly, but I was going to take care not to get it. This place was too good to lose, for me and Elsie too.

And then it was time for 'supper', which was cold potatoes and the goat's cheese, not yellow and sour like the old cheese from England in the storehouse, but white and soft. And we could eat all we wanted, even the cheese. Let me tell you, cheese tastes better when it ain't wriggling.

And then Mrs Johnson tried to get Elsie to talk, but Elsie just shook her head. And Mr Johnson prayed again. And then we went to bed.

CHAPTER 5

Two Mysteries

I couldn't sleep. I tried to tell myself it was because I ate all that food. But it wasn't. I'd never slept alone before, except that one night without Ma after she died, before I found Elsie.

At last I got up, and went out to the privy. The moonlight shone on a white path made of crushed shells, so it was easy to see the way in the starlight without a candle. Even the privy here didn't stink. Sally had told me to put down wood ash whenever I used it, to stop the flies and smells.

I finished my business and stepped outside again. The breeze from the harbour was cool. A bird hooted back in the bush. At least I hoped it was a bird, and not an Indian ghost. Clothes flapped on the line. One of them was Elsie's old dress. Now that it was clean I could see it was pink.

How had Elsie come by a pink dress? She had to have come on the convict ships. There weren't any white people in the whole land till we'd come here, and there had been no ships since. Convicts and their children only had the clothes we were given on the ships, all white or grey and checked jackets to begin with, but stained and mud coloured now.

Was Elsie the daughter of a soldier? I shook my head in the darkness. I'd thought about this before, trying to solve the mystery of where she'd come from. If Elsie was a soldier's or convict's daughter, I'd have seen her about the colony. There were so few of us you saw everyone sooner or later. And even if her ma and pa had died, the soldiers looked after their friends' families too.

So why hadn't I ever seen Elsie? And if she was a convict's brat, like me, how had she got a pink dress? Us convicts had been given good clothes aboard ship — I'd even had two shirts till someone nicked my other one. But none of them were pink. Colours were for rich people, or at least richer than most of us here — gentlemen's daughters or wives like Mrs Johnson.

I sat on a patch of grass by the back door. There was a lot to think about. How long could Elsie and I stay here? I'd work hard for a safe bed and food for the two of us. But I was ten and small. And I ate a lot. Mr Johnson would be better off with a big convict man than me to dig his garden.

But the black girl lived here, like she was their daughter. The Johnsons didn't seem to have children of their own. Maybe ... maybe they'd adopt me and Elsie ...

No. Ladies and gentlemen like the Johnsons don't go around adopting boys like me, even if they let servants eat at the table with them. But Elsie?

Elsie wasn't pretty like Abaroo, even now she was all cleaned up. She was as thin as a stick with the wood shaved off, and her face all pointy from hunger. But she used her knife and fork like a lady.

The back door opened. In the dark I could see a white face and a white petticoat. Elsie.

'Hoy,' I said. 'You ain't running off, are you?'

I was never sure how much Elsie understood, but she understood that. She pointed down to the privy.

'Well, good. This is a right good bunk we've got here. Need to make the most of it.'

I heard Elsie's feet go down to the privy. The privy door shut, then opened again. Then *plunk*, she sat beside me.

She leaned against me. It was just habit, because we had curled up together for warmth before, though tonight was hot.

'You all right?'

She didn't answer. Elsie never answered. She didn't even nod. But I could see her face in the moonlight and it didn't look frightened. Elsie was sitting out in the open and not even trembling.

Another face appeared at the door and looked out. A dark one. Abaroo wore a white petticoat too. Her bare feet were soft on the grass as she walked over and sat next to us.

I felt a bit lost, with her being so dark, so pretty and so strange. At last I said, 'It was you, weren't it? You threw the stone at that convict to stop him catching me. You followed me. You brought Mr Johnson to get us.'

'Yes. I find you.' Her voice sounded like Mrs Johnson's, like a lady's. I supposed she'd copied Mrs Johnson's way of speaking. But her voice was husky, and sort of *singing*. I thought of the black and white bird that sang in the strange tall trees. Abaroo's voice was as pretty as that bird's.

'Why did you bring Mr Johnson to us?' Hadn't she realised that if the Johnsons wanted children in their house, they might tell her to go if they had us?

Abaroo laughed. She didn't answer. Elsie sat very still next to me, listening.

'Why they take us?' I demanded. 'We're just two more mouths to feed.' A man with three vegetable gardens in the colony was rich. But even three vegetable gardens couldn't feed the whole colony, and Mr Johnson had a wife and a baby coming to feed too.

Abaroo paused, as if she was working out my words and what to say. At last she said, 'Good people. They share makes happy.' She screwed up her face. 'The be re al gal —' (I think that's what she said) '— are not share people.'

'Be re al gal,' I said slowly. 'Is that us? White people?'

Abaroo nodded.

Well, she had that right. Most be re al gal in the colony would rather steal than share. They'd been sent here *because* they were thieves. This might have been the convicts' second chance, but most didn't seem to want to take it.

'Do you … do you think Mr Johnson'll let us stay?' I felt Elsie go stiff next to me and begin to tremble. It would be hard to go back to our hut after this.

Abaroo looked at me and Elsie as if she'd never thought that they might not. 'Yes.' She sounded so certain I felt like a big rock had fallen off me. Beside me, Elsie relaxed too.

'Well,' I said. 'We better go inside.' I helped Elsie to her feet. And then I said, 'Thank you, Abaroo.'

It was hard, thanking a girl, a black girl. I'd never got into the habit of thanking people before, even Ma, though when we buried her, I wished I had. I didn't even like to think how much I was thanking this girl for now. For our lives, maybe.

She looked at me for a moment, then laughed. 'My name not Abaroo.'

'But Mr Johnson said it was.'

'My name …' She said something so fast it was hard to catch.

'Dibrung?'

She said the sounds again.

'Birrung?'

She looked at me, as if I hadn't quite got it right, but she knew I wasn't going to, no matter how many times

42

she said it. I reckoned Birrung was closer to her real name than Abaroo, anyhow. And then I thought: The native gibber must be another language. People use different words in other countries, don't they? I'd never thought the Indians could have a language; reckoned they just made sounds like birds.

If Abaroo — Birrung — had a language, I could learn it. She and I could talk together and no one else would understand.

It was too much to think about. Too much had happened in one day.

Abaroo — Birrung — took Elsie's hand. I watched the two girls go inside. And above us the moon seemed to sing a lullaby, just like Ma had done, as it played among the clouds.

CHAPTER 6

Staying Put

So we stayed there, Elsie and me.

It wasn't all potatoes and goat's cheese and clean sheets every week. (I'd never even slept in sheets. Me, Barney Bean, in sheets!)

There was hard work too, digging up tussocks to make new garden beds and learning what was a weed. Turned out that's what Mr Johnson's garden magic was — hard work, watering and weeding, when most in the colony just hoped someone else would do the hard stuff and the rain would come from the sky.

Mr Johnson didn't whip me even when I pulled out baby cabbages by mistake. He just showed me how to put them in again and give them a drink of water to 'settle them back', his voice all kind and gentle like he enjoyed teaching me.

Learning about plants was as interesting as I thought it would be. Who'd have thought a giant orange carrot could grow from a seed like a speck of dust? Or that potatoes grew under the ground and you had to dig them up? I wondered who was the first person who ever thought of digging up the ground to see if there was food under there.

But there were other things to learn too, indoor stuff, that weren't so interesting. Mrs Johnson looked sweet and gentle, but she had iron inside her too. When she asked me to do something, it got done. How to speak and hold my knife and fork and not to swear, which was hard because I didn't even know I *was* swearing back then. And how to read words on a slate then in the books, and learn the stories about God and Jesus and the others.

But the stories were good when she read them to us, especially the smiting bits, and Roman swords, and this one where Jesus turned two fish and five loaves of bread into enough food to feed a multitude. That is still one of my favourite stories, that one. We could have used Jesus in the colony. Mr Johnson said He was always there, but I can't say I noticed Him around much, except in the clergyman's house. But I never said that to Mr and Mrs Johnson.

Elsie learned her letters too, faster than I did, so fast I wondered if she already knew them. Her writing on the slate was all neat and curled, not snail tracks on a cabbage leaf like mine. Elsie was getting stronger every day, with all the potatoes and scrambled eggs and stews. Seemed she knew how to do a lot of things now she had food in her belly and was in a proper house. She could stir pots without being shown how and scrub floors and even take up the hem of the dress Mrs Johnson gave her so it didn't drag on the ground.

Elsie could peel a potato too. I'd never even known that gentlefolk like the skin off; and, as for peeling, I nearly cut my thumb off the first time I tried. Mrs Johnson was teaching Elsie to cook, not just pease pudding and boiled cabbage, but gentlefolk's foods like pancakes, with our flour ration (Mr Johnson got Elsie a ration now too) and eggs from our hens and milk from the goats.

Elsie could make goat's cheese now, and goat's-milk yeast, to make the damper light, and a fish stew with potatoes and herbs from the garden that was so good it could knock your stockings off. Mrs Johnson was teaching Sally more cooking too, because Sally had been a maid, not a cook or even scullery maid, before she'd done whatever crime had got her sent to New South Wales.

But Elsie still didn't speak, no matter how much Mrs Johnson coaxed her.

It was grand to sleep in a bed, to eat all I wanted. More than grand not to be scared all the time, to know Elsie didn't have to be scared any more either. But living with Birrung was best of all. Every morning when I woke up, I thought: There's going to be breakfast. Then my second thought was: Birrung will be there.

Birrung laughed all the time. Laughed at the men digging clay next door. Laughed when Mr Johnson brought in basket after basket of cucumbers, and got us to count them, which was a clever way of getting me to work out how to count to two thousand, because that was how many cucumbers there were. I learned how to eat cucumbers too. Ma and me had never eaten this 'salad' stuff that the Johnsons liked so much, sliced cucumbers and lettuce leaves not cooked at all, but eaten with goat's cheese crumbled on top. I made a face first time I tried it. Took me a few mouthfuls to realise it was good — and Birrung laughed.

Birrung laughed at me too when I stared as she grabbed a big lizard by its tail and bashed it against a tree. Then I laughed when Sally screamed when Birrung took the lizard into the house, and wanted to roast it on the cook fire.

Birrung was like one of Mr Johnson's miracles. The whole colony was gloomy those days, stores running low and hard work they weren't used to, and strange trees and summer when it should be winter. Even Mr and Mrs Johnson didn't laugh much, especially as the baby Mrs Johnson was going to have got bigger. Mostly they looked tired, and sometimes a bit scared too, though they tried not to let us see it.

But Birrung laughed. No matter how weary Mr Johnson was after shouting a sermon in the wind, he smiled when Birrung laughed. We all did.

And whenever I got sunburnt picking corn, or a splinter in my finger splitting wood for Sally's cook fire, or missed Ma worse than usual, I'd think: Birrung has lost her family too. Lost her whole people. If she can laugh, then I can too.

Sometimes Birrung was just gone, all alone like when she first saw me. Don't think she told Mrs Johnson she was going either. She just went. But she came back, bringing a fish or basket of native berries and once a big wild duck. Tasted good, that duck, but the berries were bitter, though I ate them because they came from her.

Christmas came, so hot the rocks felt like hearthstones.

Just about everyone in the colony turned up for Mr Johnson's sermon on Christmas Day, except for Sally, who stayed at home to watch the cooking pot, with the big frying pan out ready to bash any convict who tried to help himself to our Christmas dinner.

We sang hymns under the gum trees, almost louder than the big black beetle things that shrilled in the branches, and the seagulls that yelled on the harbour. I sat between Elsie and Birrung, in her blue and white dress. Birrung sang bits of the hymns too, and when we got to the Lord's Prayer, she knew every word.

I thought Mr and Mrs Johnson would have had Christmas dinner with the governor and the officers, but instead they walked back with me and Elsie and Birrung and one of the officers, Mr Dawes. Mr Dawes had just come back from trying to find a way to the big blue mountains in the distance, but he hadn't found it. He was as brown as a walnut.

We passed the new storehouse, with a tiled roof so thieves couldn't get in and steal the rations. The sun was right above us now, so hot the air shimmered like it was melting. The harbour waves went *slap slop* against the rocks and sand.

Birrung laughed. She pulled the blue dress over her head and then her petticoat too. She dived into the water as bare as the officers' cheeks when they'd shaved for Sundays.

'Abaroo!' cried Mrs Johnson.

I didn't know where to look. I'd never seen a girl without clothes on before. The native women had been too far away when we'd first come here for me to get a look at them. I'd never seen anyone without clothes on, except me. I shouldn't stare. But what if Birrung was drowning …

Birrung wasn't drowning. She popped up, her hair all pulled straight by the water. She held up a couple of mussels in their shells, and threw them onto the tiny beach by our feet, then dived under again.

'You must excuse her …' Mr Johnson started to say to Mr Dawes.

Mr Dawes smiled. 'There is nothing to excuse. She is too innocent to know nakedness is a sin.'

'Abaroo likes play more than study,' said Mr Johnson.

I looked at Birrung, spearing through the water. I'd

never seen anyone swim before either, then flushed because everyone else had seen me staring at her.

Elsie gave a tug on my hand as though to say, 'Come on.' Elsie had got fatter since we had been at the Johnsons'. She didn't look so much like a skinned rat now.

'Why do you call her Abaroo?' I asked Mr Johnson.

Mr Johnson looked surprised. 'That's her name.'

'No, it ain't. It's Birrung. She told me.'

Mr Johnson smiled. 'It's a heathen name. We must put it into the King's English as best we can.'

I looked around. The king owned all this, the whole colony, even though he'd never seen it. The big patch of corn, the beans, the melons and potatoes, the falling-down huts, the blue waves dancing on the harbour. And he owned the words we spoke too.

Birrung threw another mussel onto the sand.

'I'll wait with her here,' said Mrs Johnson. She lowered herself down onto the tussocks under a tree. Her belly was real big now. She looked tired, like she could do with a rest before climbing the hill.

'Are you all right, my dear?' asked Mr Johnson quietly.

She smiled at him and nodded.

So the rest of us walked up the hill. 'Have we got Sunday school today?' I asked.

I knew we hadn't. I just wanted something to say, in case I looked awkward after staring at Birrung with no clothes on. After-church school was just for Sundays, when no one worked and had free time to learn to read and write and do their sums. Sometimes there were more than fifty people with me and Elsie, writing on one of Mr Johnson's slates or with Mrs Johnson helping them read the easy bits in one of their books.

'Today is a holiday,' said Mr Johnson. 'A true "holy" day. Did you know that is where the word "holiday" comes from? No one has work today. No hangings,' Mr Johnson added softly. Mr Johnson was always quiet when he came back from praying with the men going to be hanged. 'A day of rest for all of us.'

Except you've had to give a sermon, I thought. Mr Johnson really did like praying and stuff, but it was hard work giving one of his sermons, harder even than digging in the garden. He had to shout loud enough for more than a thousand people to hear him out of doors, leading the hymns and things.

And it wasn't a day of rest for the convict on lookout on the headland, who had to make sure a supply ship didn't go straight past our harbour to Botany Bay, which is where the people back in England thought we were.

If that ship went to Botany Bay and found no trace of a settlement, they'd think we were all dead and vanished and sail away again.

And it wasn't a day of rest for Sally, because she'd been cooking …

I cheered up at that. I'd helped Sally pluck two young roosters, and helped Mrs Johnson stir the plum pudding, except it didn't have plums or dried fruit in it, but grated carrots from our garden, and berries Birrung had found, and honey that dripped from the honeycomb Birrung had brought back. Christmas dinner! Even at the governor's table they wouldn't eat finer than us.

It was more than fine. Sally cooked Mrs Johnson's recipes real well, for all she was a convict. Sally said it had been the drink that made her go bad back in England. There wasn't much alcohol left in the colony — and none for the likes of Sally — so she didn't have a chance to be bad again.

Oh, that dinner. The two roosters stuffed with damper crumbs and herbs from the garden, basted on a spit over the fire. Peeled potatoes roasted in pig fat in the Dutch oven and left to keep warm on the hearth. I'd never had potatoes all crisp like that before. Radishes and lettuces and cucumbers with goat's-cheese dressing, and peas and beans from the garden, and no one made a joke about my name as we ate them. Mrs Johnson told funny stories about her family growing up, and Mr Johnson said how when he was eight years old 'someone' let a mouse go while everyone was singing a hymn and all the women screamed and jumped up on the pews. I tried to think of any funny things in prison or on the ship, but there weren't none. So I told them about how the first time Ma went behind a bush here in New South Wales and lifted up her skirts a bird laughed at her and she got angry, thinking a convict bloke had seen her bare bottom.

'You show yourself, you blaggard!' she'd yelled, while above the bird laughed and laughed, and me too.

'We don't talk of things like that at the table,' said Mrs Johnson. But she was smiling too.

After that we ate the plum pudding, with goat's-milk custard all yellow from the eggs, and sarsaparilla tea to drink, made from the pink flowers up on the hill that Mrs Johnson had picked and dried. It was just the seven of us. The convict men only ate dinner with us when they were working.

'And a surprise for you all,' said Mr Johnson, as Mrs Johnson poured out the tea.

He smiled as he went out to the storeroom where I slept. I wondered what it could be. It couldn't be big, or I'd have seen it.

It was a small sack, just like the others we hung from the ceiling to stop the rats eating the stuff inside. Mr Johnson opened the sack over by the bench. He poured some small dark red things into a bowl, and then put something orange on a plate with a knife. He carried them over to us.

Mr Dawes stared. 'Cherries! And a tangerine!'

I looked at them curiously. I'd heard of cherries and tangerines, but never eaten any.

'The first fruits of our orchard,' Mr Johnson said proudly. 'It was worth bringing good-sized trees from the Cape.' The tangerine was a bit withered — he'd kept it especially for Christmas. He cut each of us a thin slice. It was funny, sweet and sour at the same time, but I'd have liked to eat more. We got eight cherries each, and they were even better.

I looked at the table with its cloth and empty platters and the rooster bones — I'd chew those after everyone else had gone to bed, if Sally didn't beat me to them — and thought about my happy belly and Elsie safe here next to me, not smiling but not looking scared either, and most of all Birrung, so pretty and smiling in her blue and white dress, her hair still wet from the sea.

I thought: Who would ever believe that Barney Bean would be sitting and laughing with gentlefolk?

And when Mr Johnson bowed his head to give thanks again for the bounty God had given us, I think I almost understood.

CHAPTER 7

My Brilliant Idea

Mr Johnson gave me one of his books to read after Christmas dinner. He had thousands of books, not just the ones on the shelves inside, but kept in sea chests in the shed so they didn't get wet when the roof leaked. He had brought enough books from England for every convict to borrow six at once, but he had to teach the convicts to read first.

I looked at the book. I couldn't even read the first word. I pointed to it.

Mr Johnson smiled. '*Dissuasions from Stealing.*'

'I ain't a thief!' I said. I waited for Mr Johnson to say that Ma had been one — just about every convict here had been a thief. Truth is, I'd been too young when Ma was put in prison to know if she'd stolen anything or not. I hadn't asked either. All I knew was that Ma had done her best to keep me fed.

He didn't. He gave me a book about not swearing instead. That sounded more interesting — there might have been swear words I didn't know — but it was too hard for me to read. I pretended though, in case he sent me to fetch water for Sally and Elsie to wash the plates and pots, just enjoying sitting there, glancing up at Mrs Johnson and Birrung in her pretty dress reading their books too.

That's when I got the idea.

I waited till it was growing dark and everyone went to bed. It didn't get dark till late, being midsummer, so I had a long while to wait. Mrs Johnson and Sally and Elsie sewed after supper, and Mr Johnson went down to the hospital to take the sick people the remains of our plum pudding. I'd wanted it for breakfast, but then I thought about Mr Johnson telling us to be grateful for all our good things every time he said grace before a meal, and I tried to be glad I hadn't had my foot chopped off or my head bashed in, like the folks in hospital had.

Mr Johnson came back around the cove just as it was getting dark. He said the evening prayers. We went to bed except I didn't get undressed. I snuck around, next to the lean-to where Elsie slept with Sally and Birrung. Soon as I heard Sally's snores, I tapped on the door.

Footsteps sounded on the dirt floor. Elsie peered out, in her petticoat. I beckoned her out onto the grass. She sat cross-legged, with her hands in her lap, and looked at me curiously.

I handed her the slate Mr Johnson had lent me to practise writing on.

That was my brilliant idea. Elsie was as good at her letters as Birrung. 'How about you write your name?'

Elsie stared at me. She picked up the chalk and wrote something.

Excitement prickled me like the thorns in the summer grass. I waited till she finished and handed me the slate, then looked down.

'E … l … s … i … e.' I shook my head. 'I meant write down your *real* name.'

Elsie pointed to the word on the slate.

'I know that's your name now. But what was it afore I met you?'

Elsie pointed to the word on the slate again. I looked at her, frustrated. Did she mean that her name really had been Elsie all along? I'd met two other Elsies, and three Sallys too, so I supposed it might have been.

'What about your last name?'

Elsie took back the slate.

Ah, I thought. Now we were getting somewhere. If she wrote *Smith* or *Ramsbottom*, then I could ask Mr Johnson to look up the colony records to see who her ma was, or her pa if he'd been a soldier or one of the sailors who had brought the ships here, then sailed off.

Elsie wrote slowly on the slate. She gave me a funny look, and handed the slate back to me.

It took me a bit to work out what it meant. Like I said, Elsie was better than me at her letters.

'*Noname,*' I read out loud. Elsie had written it like it was all one word, like 'Noname' really might have been her last name.

Except no one was called Noname.

I looked back at Elsie. She crossed her arms at me, and put her chin out. I knew that look. I wasn't going to get no other name than that from her. Elsie was stubborn.

But so was I. If she wouldn't tell me her real name, then I'd ask other questions.

I reckoned I had to keep them simple, so she could write *yes* or *no*. That way I'd be able to read them too.

'Are you a convict?'

Elsie's writing was slow and careful. *No.*

'Is your pa a soldier?'

This time she shook her head, just like she had when I first found her. I didn't know if she was saying, 'No, he's not a soldier,' or, 'I'm not going to answer,' or even, 'I don't know.'

'Is he a sailor?'

Elsie stared at me in the starlight. She seemed to think. She picked up the slate again and scratched on it. My heart began to beat faster. This was longer than *yes* or *no*. It had to be a proper answer! Maybe even her pa's name, and the name of his ship! Because every single person in New South Wales was a convict or a soldier or a sailor, or the son or daughter of one, except for Mr and Mrs Johnson. Even the governor and surgeon worked for the navy. The only other people were the Indians. Elsie was tanned from the sun — we all were. But you only had to glance at her to know she wasn't an Indian.

She handed me the slate again. I concentrated, making out the words. Then my excitement drained away, like the custard from the jug at dinnertime. She'd written *Is Birrung prettier than me?*

I looked at her, irritated. We'd been through a lot together, Elsie and me. I had a right to know who she was! And instead of telling me now we had a chance, she asked a stupid question like that.

'Of course Birrung is prettier than you,' I said.

Elsie scrambled to her feet, glaring down at me.

'What's wrong?' I asked. 'I'm only trying to find out —'

I stopped as Elsie stamped into the lean-to. She slammed the door. Sally asked sleepily, 'What is it?' Then I heard her snores again.

I sat there on the ground, trying to work out why Elsie was angry. Of course Birrung was prettier than Elsie. Birrung was older, taller. Elsie was just a little girl. Maybe when Elsie got a bit fatter and taller and grown up, she'd be pretty …

Above me the big bats flapped past, one lot and then another, like the waves in the harbour. There'd been clouds of bats each night ever since it had got hot and dry in spring. No one knew where they came from, but now they hung upside down in the native fig trees in the gullies, then flew off at night.

And then I thought: Maybe Birrung knows where the bats came from. Birrung knows where to find berries. I've never seen fingers move as quickly as hers when she was making a grass basket. I bet she knows where the bats come from too, and where they go each night.

But I never asked her.

Summer grew hotter, so hot even the flies rested till the cool south wind blew in each afternoon, bringing storms most weeks, with enough rain so I didn't have to carry water to the vegetables.

I had to work hard even so. We all did, at Mr Johnson's anyway, though most in the colony were still as lazy as before, the soldiers and the convicts too, just eating their rations from the storehouse and grumbling.

Still no ship had arrived from England, even though we'd been here two years. Had they sunk? Or had everyone in England forgotten they'd sent us here, across the world?

Mr Johnson's household wasn't going to starve, not with the three big gardens and his hens hatching so many chickens we had to build another pen to keep them safely locked up at night away from the native dogs. I brought the goats and sheep into a pen each night too. But rations got reduced again and the convicts' working hours too, so they could spend the extra time working in their own gardens to grow more food.

Except most of them didn't. They just spent more time trying to steal from others.

But we had a harvest to bring in. The men assigned to Mr Johnson were working less, so he and I had to work all the more. The governor also sent Mr Johnson out twice a week to supervise the convict fishermen, and Mr Johnson had his other work. He went down to Rose Hill every week now too to give a sermon there and pray with people, a whole day to get there and a day to come back.

So it was mostly me, picking melons and cucumbers and stripping corncobs from the stalk.

Then Birrung started to help me, even though she was a girl, then Elsie — she was almost as strong as Birrung now with all the good feeding — and Mrs Johnson picked the runner beans with us, the ones with the pink and black seeds for drying to eat in winter, though Mrs Johnson was what Sally called 'delicate' right now, her baby so close to being born she had to wear her apron loose, and got giddy sometimes when the sun sucked all the coolness from the world.

I wore one of Mr Johnson's hats, and Elsie wore an old hat of Mrs Johnson's, but Birrung worked with a bare head, and laughed when me and Elsie's skin peeled in long strips after we got sunburnt, like bark peeling off the native trees.

Mr and Mrs Johnson never said they were worried about no ship arriving, or even about the baby coming. But I knew they must be. Just about all the women I knew who'd had a baby in prison died, or their baby did. I knew lots of women didn't die or none of us would be here. But you could see Mr Johnson didn't like leaving Mrs Johnson now, even just to visit the sick.

And still no ship came.

CHAPTER 8

The Screams in the Night

March 1790

The scream woke me.

It was a hot night. My shirt stuck to my back on my bed. The damp cabbage-tree walls seemed to breathe out moisture. There'd been a storm and the whole building was still damp.

I ran out of my storeroom lean-to into the house. Birrung looked out of the other lean-to, with Elsie behind her. Sally pushed past them, holding up a slush lamp, a wick floating in sheep fat. 'You go back to sleep,' she told us.

The scream came again.

Mr Johnson appeared at the bedroom door, holding a candlestick. He looked scared. I hadn't ever seen Mr Johnson scared like that. 'It's Mrs Johnson,' he began.

'Better boil some water, sir,' said Sally. She looked at me. 'You help him. You two,' she repeated to Elsie and Birrung, 'go back to sleep.'

'No,' said Birrung. 'I help.'

Mr Johnson hesitated.

Sally pushed Birrung away. 'This is no place for you, girl. Nor Elsie neither.' She went into the Johnsons' bedroom, the slush lamp in her hand.

'Do as you're told,' said Mr Johnson quietly to Birrung.

'I stay,' said Birrung softly. Elsie took her hand and just stood there too.

Mr Johnson didn't say anything more. He just put sticks on the fire. The coals flared. I took the candle and went outside to get a bucket of water from the well. When I came back, Elsie and Birrung sat by the fire. Elsie looked frightened. Mr Johnson was praying silently. Birrung's face was a shadow in the firelight.

I put the candle down and poured the water into the pot and hung it in the fireplace. Mrs Johnson groaned in the bedroom, then she screamed again.

'Go to bed,' I told Elsie. She shook her head. Like I said, Elsie was stubborn.

'Amen,' said Mr Johnson. He looked up from his prayer. 'God protect my wife,' he whispered. 'When we first landed, we had a son. He was born dead. So small he was. So still. Mrs Johnson was ill. I thought she might die too. I would be alone in a strange land ...'

Another scream came from the bedroom.

'No,' said Birrung. She stood up. She said more, in her own language, like a song from the black and white birds that sang in the mornings. She took the candle and went out to her lean-to bedroom. I thought she had decided to obey and go back to bed. But she returned with the grass basket she kept by her bed. Sally had told me there was a chip of stone in there and some dried toadstools and a few dried leaves. Rubbish things, said Sally, but Birrung wouldn't throw them away.

Now Birrung took the basket into Mrs Johnson's bedroom.

Mrs Johnson cried out again. I heard Sally's voice, angry. I heard Birrung, stern with lots of words, some I could understand and unclear ones too. I had never heard Birrung talk like that, not laughing at all.

The water steamed in the pot. Mr Johnson prayed again, quiet, by the fire. I wondered if I should pray as well. But why would God answer me if He didn't answer Mr Johnson?

I clasped my hands and shut my eyes anyway. Please, God, I prayed. Let Mr Johnson and Mrs Johnson have a baby who stays alive. They have been father and mother to us all. Give them a baby now.

A sweet smoke smell came from the bedroom. I realised I hadn't heard Mrs Johnson cry out for a while.

Was she all right? Was she … dead? I thought of the woman who'd died on the ship, her body thrown overboard and her dead baby too. Made me wonder how the world still had people in it, so many women and their babies dying.

'Amen,' I whispered hurriedly, like Mr Johnson had taught me to when I came to the end of a prayer. I looked at his face, tight and white in the firelight.

Elsie put her hand in mine. I held it, hard. It was almost like we had been last year, the two of us close for comfort.

We sat there, the three of us, the fire flickering, the pot steaming. None of us said anything. I think I was as close to Elsie and Mr Johnson that night as I have ever been to anyone, the three of us hoping and praying so hard for the same thing that we had no need for words.

I heard a shout in the bedroom. It was Sally's voice, I thought. Or was it? Someone laughed in triumph. Birrung? Why would Birrung laugh now?

There was only one reason I could think of. I squeezed Elsie's hand harder, and she squeezed back.

Mr Johnson stared at the bedroom door. His lips moved again in a silent prayer.

A baby cried, a sort of choke at first, and then a wail.

Sally looked out of the room. 'Hot water,' she ordered, just like she was the mistress, and Mr Johnson the servant. Then she smiled and said, 'You have a daughter.'

Mr Johnson cried out, but not to Sally or to me. Maybe he cried to God. He grabbed the pot and ran into the room.

Smoke came from the bedroom, funny smoke that made me feel like I wasn't quite there, as if the hut had floated into another land.

At last the door opened again. Mr Johnson came out, with a baby wrapped in a blanket. He looked red-eyed. The baby had a red face too. He sat on the splintery chair by the fire, and looked at the tiny baby. Looked and looked, like he'd never seen anything so lovely. 'God has not forgotten us,' he whispered. 'Even if England has.'

I got up, and Elsie too, still holding my hand. I peered at the baby. She wasn't lovely at all. Her face was all crumpled and screwed up. She looked a bit angry, as if she was saying, 'What have you brought me to?'

'She's got no hair!' I said, before I could stop myself. Poor Mr and Mrs Johnson, going through so much and getting a bald daughter!

Elsie let go of my hand and gave me a sharp elbow in the ribs.

Mr Johnson didn't even glance up. 'Babies often don't have any hair,' he murmured. 'It will grow. She will grow. She will be tall and happy ...' His voice died away. His eyes shut, like he was asleep, but he still held the baby close to him.

It was getting light. Sunbeams danced through a crack in the wall. Down at the barracks the drum rolled, telling the convicts to get up and go to work. I opened the shutters and glanced back into the bedroom. Mrs Johnson lay on the bed. Her eyes were shut, but she was smiling. She was breathing too, her chest going up and down.

Birrung sat beside her, holding a big shell with smoky burning stuff in it, what I had smelled before. Birrung's basket lay on the floor next to her. Sally was doing

71

something in a corner I couldn't see. At last Birrung put the shell down. She and Sally came out. Sally shut the door behind her.

Sally picked up the frying pan. 'Potato cakes for breakfast,' she said.

Birrung began to peel and grate the potatoes without being asked. Elsie cut up the onions and beat the eggs, just as Mrs Johnson had shown her. I was embarrassed sitting in my shirt and bare legs. I went and put my trousers on. I wondered if I should put my shoes on, like it was Sunday, for the baby. But then I thought: The baby won't notice. Nor would Mr Johnson neither. And those were the only shoes I had and no chance of getting more till a ship came from England.

Mr Johnson still sat by the fire, the baby in one arm, his eyes closed, despite the noise Sally was making with the frying pan. The baby was asleep now too.

Birrung set the table quietly, plates and knives and forks and spoons.

The potato cakes smelled good, pan after pan of them fried in mutton dripping, piled up on the hearth to keep warm. Sally kept mixing and frying, and Mr Johnson sat dozing with the baby. I just wanted to get my stomach around those potato cakes.

At last Sally said loudly, 'Breakfast's ready.'

Mr Johnson opened his eyes. Sally smiled. She didn't often smile like that. 'What name have you given her, sir?'

'Milbah,' said Birrung softly.

Sally glared at her, like she hadn't forgiven her for taking charge in the bedroom. 'What name have you given her, sir?' she repeated.

Mr Johnson looked down at the baby again. 'Her name is Milbah.'

Sally glanced at Birrung, then at him. 'But that's a native name.'

'Yes,' said Mr Johnson. 'My daughter is Milbah Maria Johnson.'

And he looked at Birrung like she was his daughter as well, looked at her with so much love that I knew it was all right that I loved Birrung too.

CHAPTER 9

The Brother

The young man came to get Birrung a week later.

Heat sucked at the leaves of the lettuce and cucumber plants, row after row of them limp on the neatly turned soil. I'd been lugging buckets of water to the vegetables since dawn. Only the watermelons and the corn looked happy, over a hundred melons on the vines and more than an acre of corn, each plant with four to six fat cobs. The melons were bigger than my head. Later I'd have to go to the other plots to water the pumpkins and the fruit trees.

No one had stolen anything from Mr Johnson's gardens yet. Mr Johnson kept crops like corn and potatoes that were easy to steal near the house. The convicts couldn't steal the fruit, because the trees were too small to give much yet, and a ripe pumpkin was too big for a man to carry away unnoticed, so it was safe to leave them unguarded.

Down at the other end of the garden Elsie picked beans and carrots and turnips for our dinner. The convict men, Old Tom and Scruggins, were off digging pails of pig manure to feed the garden. These were different convicts from the men we'd had before, because the others had kept on swearing in front of Mrs Johnson. Even when she warned they'd get no more corn and potatoes if they used bad language, they kept on swearing so much I wondered if they knew other words to say.

Pig manure stank. The garden would stink too, but Mr Johnson said that muck and manure grew good vegetables. Old Tom and Scruggins would stink as well, after getting the manure, but they stank anyway. I don't think they'd ever had a bath in their lives, except when they'd been scrubbed when they came aboard the ships that brought us here.

Mr Johnson came out with Birrung. He said, 'Abaroo says Mrs Johnson must have oysters to make her strong.'

Birrung laughed and nodded. I thought: Birrung wants to go down to the beach again. She wants to swim without any clothes on in the waves. I felt my face grow hot.

Elsie looked out the back door. Mr Johnson said, 'We're going oyster gathering. Will you come with us?'

Elsie looked at me. She looked at Birrung. She shook her head and went back inside.

We hadn't even got past the garden though when Mr Johnson stopped. A black man was walking up the track, a real wild Indian. He didn't even wear clothes like some natives did, including Bennelong, who was friends with the governor. There had been more of them around lately. They hadn't all died in the plague except for Birrung and Nanberry, like we'd thought, just moved away for a while. This native carried two spears, with big sharp barbs.

'Go inside,' said Mr Johnson quietly to me and Birrung.

I turned to go. Birrung stayed where she was.

I hesitated.

'Go,' said Mr Johnson. I went, but just to the door. I peered outside.

The three of them talked, the Indian man and Mr Johnson and Birrung. They seemed angry, every one of them.

I thought: If the black man hurts Birrung or Mr Johnson with his spear, I'll …

I wondered what I could do. Mr Johnson didn't even have a musket, like the soldiers had. Then I thought of the big frying pan. I ran across the room and grabbed it, ignoring Sally's and Elsie's stares.

'What is it?' cried Mrs Johnson from the bedroom as I ran outside.

I was too late. The black man was walking back down the track, away from us. Birrung ran past me into the house. Her face was wet and all scrunched up.

I wanted to hug her, to tell her not to cry. But I just stepped back, holding the frying pan and feeling silly.

Mr Johnson walked slowly back to the house. He looked at the pan in my hand. 'What's that for?'

'In case the Indian hurt you,' I said.

Mr Johnson smiled and shook his head. 'They were fishing spears, not fighting spears.'

I hadn't even known that there were different types. 'What did he want?'

'Abaroo,' said Mr Johnson.

I felt anger sweep up from my toes. The black man had seen how pretty she was. He wanted Birrung to be his wife …

'He is her brother,' said Mr Johnson quietly. 'Abaroo wanted to go with him, to live with her father, Maugoran, or with Barangaroo, the wife of Bennelong. I told her she must stay here. We must try to teach her to be civilised, to know God ...'

To help Mrs Johnson if she gets sick, I thought. Sometimes women did get sick afterwards, even if they didn't die when they had the baby. Childbirth fever, they called it. That's what had killed lots of the women who had babies back in gaol. But maybe Birrung knew how to make that better too ...

'I didn't know she had any family,' I said. 'I thought they all died in the plague.' It felt funny, to think that all along she'd had family. I'd thought she was an orphan like me.

'They left her to die when she was sick! We are her family now. She must stay here,' said Mr Johnson. He hesitated. 'The governor wishes her to stay too. Barney, perhaps I shouldn't tell a child this ...'

A child, I thought. I'm ten years old! I've sailed across the world! And stayed alive in Newgate Prison, which was harder.

'There've been more attacks by the natives. Even people killed. The natives have been sadly provoked,

I know, but … well, the governor hopes Abaroo, like Bennelong and little Nanberry, might be an ambassador to their people. Teach them to like us …'

By keeping Birrung away from her pa and brother? I thought. By keeping Bennelong prisoner? It was a funny way to make friends.

'And to know the ways of God,' finished Mr Johnson.

I looked down as Elsie's hand took the frying pan from mine. Back in the lean-to I could hear Birrung sobbing.

CHAPTER 10

Birrung Stays

April 1790

Birrung didn't go. It would have been easy to leave us, to leave our house, to leave the colony. The colony was a prison without any walls. Any of the convicts could have wandered off, except they'd starve, or be killed by the natives.

Birrung could have gone back to her family. She could have fished in a canoe with Barangaroo, swum every day instead of working in the garden. But she stayed with us.

The melons ripened, and more corn. We spent night after night shucking the paper husks off and cutting the kernels from the cobs, to make the crop smaller to store, me and the Johnsons and Birrung and Sally and Elsie sitting in the firelight, and baby Milbah sleeping in the cradle made from a sea chest.

When Milbah wasn't sleeping, she made a lot of noise, crying or laughing, and made messes in the napkins Sally had to wash. But her face wasn't red now — it was pink and white — and she even had a tiny curl of hair at the front. Sometimes Mrs Johnson let me hold her. She squirmed a lot, but she felt sort of nice too.

We hung the bags of corn on ropes in the shed, with sharp rounds of metal halfway down to stop the rats running up the walls and down the rope and eating all our harvest.

There were bags of dried beans and dried peas, and pumpkins and marrows left in the sun till their skins hardened so they didn't rot during the winter. Sally boiled some of the watermelons, then strained the juice till it was a sweet clear syrup, and poured it into tightly corked old wine bottles, to sweeten our puddings in the year to come. There was no sugar left in the colony now, not even treacle or molasses. Birrung hadn't brought us any honey for months — she didn't go off by herself to forage now. I wondered if it was because she had decided to stay and if she saw her family it might be too hard to leave them again.

Mr Johnson decided that this year the carrots and beetroot could stay in the ground over winter. Root vegetables didn't rot in the cold like he said they did in English winter gardens. It didn't even snow here in winter: there were just the cold winds from the south. I was glad. I'd been colder in England than I ever wanted to be again, and digging up carrots and beetroot to store was a lot of work.

Work had always been something you were supposed to try to get out of before. Work was Ma leaning over, bashing the oysters off the rocks, day after day till she said her back was crying in agony, and her hands were raw and bleeding from the shell cuts. Though Ma never shirked a day in her life, far as I knew. But working up here, with Birrung and Elsie, or Mr Johnson, or just by myself, watching the harbour and the green and red birds, thinking of all the good food in the ground and in the shed, the food I'd helped grow, I was the happiest I'd ever been. I learned that work can be one of the best things in the world. I'll never forget it was Mr Johnson who taught me that.

They were good days. Mrs Johnson held Milbah like she was a precious jewel from Araby. I felt like I did when a carrot seed and dirt turned into a crisp fat root. It was like our colony; nothing but trees yet now we had a village and gardens, though the colony stank more than Milbah did when she made a mess in her napkin. And the way Mrs Johnson smiled at Milbah and Birrung seemed to light up the house. We all laughed a lot in those days.

I was penning up the goats one afternoon after dinner, giving them each a carrot — goats need a bribe if you're to get them to go where you want them. There was one with a black foot who wouldn't go in even so. 'Get in, you b—' I said, using a word I wasn't supposed to. I heard a laugh above me. It was Birrung, sitting right up on a branch of a gum tree.

She threw down a carrot. It landed *whump* in the pen. Old Black Foot scrambled in after it. I shut the pen quickly.

'Thank you!' I called, careful not to look up again in case I saw her bare legs.

I heard a swishing sound. Birrung slid down the tree next to me. She pushed her skirts back into place and grinned at me. 'Walk?'

Go for a walk with her? Just the two of us, when Sally expected me to bring her a bucket of fresh water for the morning, when Mrs Johnson would be waiting to say evening prayers, which she did on the nights when Mr Johnson was away in Rose Hill as he was this evening?

I grinned back and nodded. I was glad Birrung was happy enough to go for a walk again. I was even gladder it was with me.

I thought we'd go down to the harbour. Maybe she'd even teach me to swim. But instead she scrambled up the hill, past the brick pits. At last we came to a big smooth boulder, sitting near the top. She sat down on it. I sat next to her, feeling the warm stone, smelling strange trees, hot and cold breezes weaving around us.

I looked at the harbour. You could see the flagpole from here. As soon as the lookout saw sails from England, they'd run a flag up the pole.

The flagpole was empty. Day after day, no matter how much everyone stared at it.

Would a ship ever come?

It'd be winter soon. We'd landed here with food for three years, but rats and humans had stolen a lot. Even the officers didn't dig their own gardens, but sat back while their convicts did it for them. Would some folk starve? The lazy ones, the ones who'd rather steal than work?

I glanced at Birrung. We wouldn't starve. Governor Phillip's garden was raided night after night. But the convicts were too grateful to Mr Johnson for helping those who were sick or in trouble, like me and Elsie, to steal from the Johnsons.

Or at least they were so far.

Birrung gestured to me to be still. I froze. I thought a snake was about to bite me — there'd been a big brown one among the corn one day till Birrung had grabbed it by the tail and lashed it down and broke its neck. I waited for this snake to put its fangs in me …

Birrung put her arms around a big old tree next to our rock, and then hugged it with her knees. It looked strange, her black legs under her petticoat. She made her way up that tree like a slug, except slugs are slow and she was fast. I thought: That must be how she climbed up the tree by the garden.

She reached into a hole and pulled out an o'possum. It hardly had time to wake before she yanked its head back, sharp, so. The head hung limp, dead.

'Meat,' said Birrung. She threw it down. I caught it. I watched her legs under her skirts as she climbed down, then flushed when she saw me watching.

She laughed. She picked up a bit of rock. Looked like any old rock to me. But she bashed it against a boulder, and then bit the edges with her sharp white teeth. And suddenly the bit of rock was like an axe blade crossed with a knife.

Birrung cut the o'possum around the neck and paws and backside, glanced at me, then went more slowly, so I could follow what she did, pushing her thumbs under the skin to take the fur off.

Meat. It had been weeks since we'd eaten fresh meat. We'd had to live on the salt pork ration, so hard Sally had to cut it into shreds so we could eat it, just two pounds a week for a grown-up and I got two-thirds of that and Elsie even less, because she was a girl. It was against the law now to kill any hens or goats or pigs or sheep to eat. They had to be kept to breed more animals.

The governor had given the officers their own shooters, convicts who had guns and powder and could bring in wild ducks and kangaroos for their masters. But when Mr Johnson had asked for a shooter too, the governor had said no, even though Mr Johnson was a gentleman, like the officers.

And now a girl had got fresh meat for us. She didn't even need a musket and lead shot and powder.

Birrung looked at me looking at her. Her hands moved again, slowly, in the grass now, showing me what to do: tearing off tussocks and sort of plaiting them — and there was a basket, to carry the meat.

I wondered if somehow Birrung could make bread for us too. I missed bread nearly as much as fresh meat. More maybe, because I'd never eaten meat much back in England, but Ma usually had a few farthings for a loaf of bread, soft white bread with a hard black crust, English bread, not Sally's heavy cornmeal damper ...

Then I realised. I didn't think of England as home. The colony wasn't just where I lived. It was where I wanted to live, with the harbour and bright birds and Elsie and Birrung, who could swim and save a baby girl and her mother and get us fresh meat ...

'Can you find wheat? You know, to make flour for bread?' I felt stupid as soon as I said it. How could a native make bread? Even Birrung?

Birrung laughed. She reached over to another tussock and shook it, and caught the tiny seeds in her hand. The palm of her hand was lighter than the back. The seeds looked black and shiny. She put them on the boulder, rubbed her rock backwards and forwards over them, then showed me the paste this made.

It didn't look like bread. She held it out for me to taste. It didn't taste like bread either. It didn't taste of anything much. But damper dough didn't taste of much till it was cooked either. Would this be like bread if it was cooked?

'You'd need a lot of them seeds to make a loaf of bread.'

I think she understood me. You never did know how much Birrung understood. She just laughed again. She threw the paste away — threw away good food, when most of the colony were wondering if they were going to starve, as if she knew food was all around her. I reckoned for her it was.

The shadows were turning into night. The first star winked at us, above the harbour. The waves turned purple with the dusk. Suddenly it was all so beautiful I never wanted to leave, sitting on this warm rock that had soaked up the sun. But we didn't have a lamp with us, or even a slushie. I said, 'We better get home. Don't want to be lost in the dark.'

Birrung nodded. She picked up the meat that had

been an o'possum. She stopped, and pointed at the star. 'Birrung,' she said softly.

'You think it's pretty?'

'No. Yes. My name is Birrung. That is birrung too.'

'You're called Birrung, like a star?'

She laughed. I'd got it right.

Now I knew another native word. I could write words. I could speak native ones …

I pointed up to the sky. 'What's that?'

'Warrigwul.'

Did she mean the sky, or the growing dark? Or maybe all the stars that were popping out through the black?

I pointed to myself.

'Wungarra,' said Birrung. She touched herself. 'Guragalungayung.'

We played the game all the way home, me pointing and her giving the Indian names. I don't think I said them right. Maybe I didn't even hear them right. Some of the sounds were strange. But she seemed happy when I tried.

The stars shone like the embroidery on Mrs Johnson's best bonnet. We made our way down through the rocks to the huts, looking at our feet. The dark had jumped up at us faster than I'd expected. I was surprised how easy it was to see my feet though and the way ahead.

I glanced up at the sky. A thousand birrungs stared back at me. Stars …

One broke away from all the rest. It darted across the sky, bright as a thin flame, then vanished, like it had dropped into the sea.

'Shooting star,' I said. 'Ma used to say you could make a wish on a shooting star.'

Birrung stared at the melting gleam where the shooting star had vanished. Her face crumpled, like a used handkerchief. 'No,' she whispered. 'That star says bad is coming. Bad, bad, bad.'

I could see the candlelight in the doorway, and Elsie's face looking out anxiously, but when she saw us, she scowled and went back in. She scowled at me a lot, those days, despite the harvest and learning how to make corn vinegar and cook dumplings so light they jumped into your mouth.

There'd be potatoes hot for us on the hearth, and maybe a scolding for being out so late, but not much of one when Mrs Johnson saw we'd brought fresh meat. And tomorrow we'd have meat stew, the one with carrots and potatoes and onions and thyme that I liked best …

Bad? Everything bad had happened already. Prison back in England, those months at sea, Ma dying, those months going hungry, the plague that killed so many of Birrung's people, and now hunger for all the other men here too.

What else bad could happen to us now?

CHAPTER 11

Death Ships

June 1790

The death ships sailed into the harbour, white sails and a blue sea, but only horror on board.

We danced as we saw them sail through the heads, me and Elsie, while Birrung looked on and laughed. The *Lady Juliana* had come a couple of weeks before, bringing us food and tools as well as more women convicts. Now there would be more people. More food, more tools. More hope that our huddle of huts might grow into a town and farms.

Mr Johnson was on one of the first boats out to the new ships. We watched as he climbed back up the hill, me and Elsie and Birrung and Mrs Johnson holding Milbah. Even Sally mixed her pudding outside today, to get a view of what was happening on the harbour: the new ships, the tiny boats being rowed out to them or back to shore. Would he bring letters from friends back home? Presents they'd sent maybe, like packets of seeds, a sewing kit (Sally had broken our last needle), bolts of cloth?

But Mr Johnson wasn't smiling as he walked up to the house, his hands empty. He looked like he'd seen the hell he talked about sometimes on Sundays.

Mrs Johnson ran to him. 'What is it, dearest?'

He held up a hand to stop his wife coming closer. 'Best not come near me. There's fever on the ships. I might give it to you, or the children. There's …' He shook his head, as though he couldn't find the words, this man who shouted out his sermons every week. 'The convicts are just lying there in the stinking dark below the decks,' he whispered. 'The dying and the dead together, while the officers laugh and joke on deck. Naked or in rags. Starved and chained below deck for near a year, no light, scarce any food, lying among the dead, the skeletons and filth.'

Mrs Johnson stared at him. 'But why? How …'

'Greed,' said Mr Johnson. 'No charity. No feeling. The captains kept the wretches' rations to sell when they got here. The convicts starved to death so the captains can grow rich. At least a quarter of them died on the way here, and most who lived will die tomorrow or next week. Infected sores from the chains, from sitting in filth and salt water for nearly a year. Blind from no sunlight. When we got the first of the prisoners to the shore, they couldn't stand, too weak to even drink. Just lay where we had left them, in a line, like blind white worms …'

Mrs Johnson handed Milbah to Sally. 'I'll get the hospital basket.' It held bandages that Sally washed and ironed every week and a lotion Surgeon White brewed from one of the native plants. 'They'll need help at the hospital.'

'No,' said Mr Johnson. 'You will stay here.' He looked at the rest of us. 'None of you will leave this house and garden until I return. You understand?'

'But —' began Mrs Johnson.

'There's disease,' said Mr Johnson quietly. He looked at Milbah, then at his wife. 'Typhus; who knows what else?' He bit his lip, then added, 'I'll sleep at the hospital so I don't carry infection back here.'

I thought Mrs Johnson would argue. But she glanced at Milbah, at Birrung and Elsie and me, and she nodded.

She kissed her hand, then blew the kiss to him. 'God be with you,' she said softly. Somehow in that moment they seemed together, even though they stood apart, and I thought: If I ever marry, I want my family to be like this.

And then I thought of the white faces down in the dark holds of those pretty ships upon the harbour, the dead and living bodies like white worms laid out on the grass. I wanted to hide up here in our garden till every one of them had got better or died, wanted to stay here where it smelled good and was safe.

'I'll come with you,' I said.

Mr Johnson shook his head. 'You're a good lad,' he said. 'You're needed here. Take care of the women.'

Then he left.

We waited, day after day. Messengers came up from the big tents they'd made into a hospital, to pick up the parcels of food we left on the doorstep. I killed three of the hens, for soup, and dug potatoes till my back felt like breaking so Sally could peel them, to feed the sick, the starving. I chopped wood to keep the cook fire going, lugged back fallen branches from the bush, and tried not to feel guilty I was safe and well fed with so many dying, tried not to resent them too, for bringing fear back into our lives, and taking Mr Johnson from us. Tried not to hear Mrs Johnson crying in her room at night for all she smiled as she led us in a hymn and prayer after supper.

One morning I came into the house early and there was Elsie, already up, frying onions in chicken fat, putting them in the big pot with layers of stale damper and goat's cheese, then pouring water on top. She put it next to the fire, where it would cook slowly, then began to mix the damper for breakfast — white wheat damper again, because the death ships had brought us stores too. We ate, just as the convicts on those ships had starved.

Sally came out, yawning and tying the ribbons of her cap under her chin. She peered into the pot. 'What's this mess you've made, girl?'

Elsie shrugged.

Sally shook her head. 'Don't see why the master had to bring a dumb girl into the house.'

'She ain't dumb!' I yelled. I think we were all on edge back then, with death so much about us. I stood in front of Sally. 'You take that back! Elsie just can't speak, that's all!'

'I'll say as I think,' said Sally.

'What's all the noise?' Mrs Johnson came out of the bedroom, where she'd been feeding Milbah. She looked at both of us as if one more angry word might make her cry again. 'The Lord tells us to love our neighbours. At times like these we should be thankful for what we have, not argue with our friends.'

'The girl has filled my good pot with some mess ...' began Sally.

Mrs Johnson made an effort to smile. She peered into the pot. 'It smells delicious,' she said.

Elsie made a face at Sally. She picked up the slate from the shelf, wrote something, and held it up. Sally made out the words slowly. '*Onion soup.* That ain't how you make onion soup, girl.'

Elsie shrugged.

I took a spoon and tasted it. 'It's the best soup I've ever ate,' I said. And it was. But soup needed roosters and vegetables to make it taste good. How had Elsie made a giant pot of soup like this with just onions and fat and water and stale damper, and without Mrs Johnson or Sally to teach her?

Elsie gave me that look that was as close to a smile as she ever came.

Birrung came in, fastening her apron. She looked at Sally who was still angry, at me indignant, at Elsie looking smug and at Mrs Johnson who was so tired, with shadows under her eyes for worry about her husband. I thought she'd do something to make us laugh. Birrung always laughed. But she just took the basket and went out to collect the eggs.

We cooked. We waited. Day after day we cooked and waited.

Mr Johnson didn't come.

I tried not to think what would happen if Mr Johnson caught the typhus. If he died, like Ma, I could keep the garden going and chop the wood. I could put on new bark to stop the roof leaking too. I could take care of us all!

Except I couldn't. And all of us in the house knew it too.

Mrs Johnson gathered every bit of cloth in the house: her petticoats, the dishcloths, my spare shirt. Everything we could spare went down to the harbour, to cover the patients' nakedness, to keep them warm, or to be ripped into bandages to cover the sores where chains had rubbed. Why did I need a spare shirt when these men had none?

I only left the house and garden once, to get some rations. Old Tom and Scruggins, who were looking after Mr Johnson's other gardens — but taking it easy, I bet — were supposed to bring rations up and leave them on the doorstep for us. But there'd been no rations on the step that morning, and we'd run out of flour. Sally said it was more than a soul could bear, all this and no bread either …

It was strange, down in the tiny town. The thin wind whispered between the mud huts. There were a few new faces, ghost people staggering about. But mostly there was no one, except on the grass by the shore where the hospital tents flapped in the wind. I could hear a long dull moaning and tried to tell myself it was the wind, not hundreds of convicts, in pain and afraid of the light, not the ghosts of their friends crying, 'How could man do this to man? How can this be?'

I stayed away from the tents, like I'd promised Mr Johnson, and even when I saw another person, I kept well away in case they had the fever and I might take it back to our house. I scrambled along the rocks above the harbour though, to see if Old Tom and Scruggins were working like they should have been.

They weren't. The bare apple and cherry trees looked dismal in the wind. But there was orange fruit on some of the trees, which meant it was ripe, and no one had pinched it, either because they respected Mr Johnson or because most convicts wouldn't eat fruit. They said it gave them the runs and stung their gums, and was too new and strange.

I half filled my bag with the really orange ones — I wasn't sure what they were. The tangerines were still green. Then I hurried over to the storehouse.

'Why, it's Barney Bean. Ain't seen you in an age. How are you growing, little bean?'

'Ha ha. Very well, sir,' I said politely. 'Can I have the rations for Mr Johnson's house?'

The storeman went in to get them just as someone spoke behind me. 'What are you doing here, boy?'

It was Scruggins. He looked tired. Huh. Tired with doing nothing while Mr Johnson was busy, I thought.

'Getting the rations because you didn't.'

'Well, I'm getting them now, ain't I?' But Scruggins sounded weary, not defensive. 'As you're here, you can do it. Saves me lugging them up the hill. Tell Mrs Johnson I'm sorry they're late.' He rubbed his whiskery face and I realised his hands were trembling. 'I were down at the tents, holding down this poor bloke while Surgeon White cut off his arm. All rotten it was. Surgeon said it was the only thing that might save him. I stayed with him till he slept. Held his other hand. Man shouldn't be alone at a time like that. I'll head back there now.'

My heart gave a little *thunk*, like it was made of stone. I'd been bad-mouthing — well, bad-thinking — Scruggins, and he'd been doing far more than me.

'Old Tom down there too?'

'Won't leave Mr Johnson's side, except to get him what he needs. You tell Mrs Johnson we see he eats, at least. Can't get him to rest. He reckons he can feed the sick and tend their bodies and pray for them at the same time. He says the Lord will give him the strength to do his duty.' Scruggins looked at me, almost man to man. 'I'll tell you what, Barney boy. Every convict in this colony thinks that man is an angel. Don't know how many lives he's saved.'

I thought: Mr Johnson saved mine too. And Elsie's.

When I got back, I took off my clothes behind the shed and scrubbed them in the trough, then scrubbed myself, over and over, till my skin was red and my hair was sticking up like a rooster's comb. One louse or flea could carry the ship's fever, could kill Elsie and Birrung and Milbah and Mrs Johnson and Sally, and me too.

Then when everything had dried in the sunlight, I dressed and went inside to help Birrung, who was peeling potatoes for more soup. She never slipped down to swim in the harbour now, or went roaming in the dusk.

It had been weeks since Birrung had laughed. Suddenly I needed to hear laughter. Birrung's laughter would drive away the shadows that flickered through me after Scruggins's words.

I took one of the potatoes and carved it into a man's face, with holes for eyes, and a pointed nose, and a big grin. I held it up to Birrung.

'Hello,' I said in a funny voice. 'I am a potato man.' I held up a carrot, and made it bow to the potato. 'Hello, Mr Potato,' I said in another voice.

Birrung laughed, just as I'd hoped she would. She picked up a long parsnip, and made it bow to the potato too, just like Mr Johnson bowed when he met the governor. 'Hello, Mr Potato,' she said in Mrs Johnson's most polite voice. 'I am Mr Parsnip.' She laughed again.

Someone made a noise behind us. I turned. Elsie stared at us from the doorway. Had she been trying to say something? I'd never heard her make a sound before, even when she cried each night the first week we were together.

'Oh, Elsie, come and —' I began.

Elsie whirled, her skirts swishing against the floor. She ran to her lean-to. In a few heartbeats she was back, Mrs Johnson's old hat on her head, and a bundle in her hand.

I stared at it. 'What's that?'

Elsie didn't answer. She marched over to the front door, and outside.

I went out the door too, and caught up with her on the path past the brick pits. 'Elsie! What are you doing?'

Elsie glared at me. She nodded down towards the huts huddled around the harbour.

'Are you taking something to Mr Johnson?'

She shook her head, then gave me a rough push on the chest. She began to march down the track again.

I caught her arm. 'Elsie, you can't go down there. You might catch the typhus.'

Elsie wrenched her arm away. And suddenly I understood. 'You want to leave the Johnsons? You've got your things in that bundle?'

Elsie nodded.

'But why? We've got it good here! And I'm learning how to grow things and Mrs Johnson is teaching you to cook.'

Elsie shrugged, her eyes on mine.

'It's dangerous down there! There's the fever and ...' Things that you shouldn't see, I thought. Because I reckoned sometime Elsie had seen too much.

Elsie waited maybe five breaths, in case I said anything more, then turned to walk away.

'No!' I said. 'Wait! If you've got to go, I'll get my things too. You can't go down there alone!' Mrs Johnson had taught Elsie enough for her to work as a cook for an officer. But she needed someone to take care of her. She needed me. Maybe, deep inside me, I knew I needed her too.

She stopped. She turned and looked at me. 'It's you and me, Elsie,' I said softly. 'Always was. Always will be. I don't understand, but if something's happened and you want to leave, just wait till I get my hat and shoes.'

Elsie smiled. It was like the moon rising out of the dark mountains. I'd never seen her smile properly like that. She put out her hand, the one that wasn't holding the bundle. I took it. She led me back inside.

Birrung had gone. I saw her sitting with Sally on a rough seat Mr Johnson had made out in the garden, plaiting onion tops together to hang them up to dry. Mrs Johnson sat in the sun too, patting Milbah's back to make her burp.

Elsie let go of my hand, then marched into the girls' lean-to. When she came back, her hands were empty.

'So we're staying here?' I asked uncertainly.

Elsie nodded. She took up the potato peeling where Birrung had left off. After a bit I joined her, making more soup for the almost dead.

I never did work out what Elsie had got upset about. Like I said, she could be stubborn.

CHAPTER 12

The Dead

Days passed in a shiver of winter. Weeks passed, bleak and cold, except in the garden, which was sheltered by the house, or our big warm room with its fire. But all through the colony the bodies stank where they'd been buried above the Tank Stream.

One morning I came down to the garden to find an arm among the potato plants. It was a woman's arm, I think, probably dug up by a dingo, maybe dropped when a sound from inside our house scared him the night before.

I didn't tell Mrs Johnson about the arm. I didn't tell anyone. I thought I'd take it back to the Tank Stream graveyard, but the dingoes might just dig it up again. So I buried it under an apple tree, and said a prayer for whoever had owned the arm, for all those white-faced wretches and for Mr Johnson trying to help.

For us all really.

And then I dug up potatoes and onions to make more soup.

At last one day Mr Johnson walked back up the hill, just as the cease-work drum roll sounded for the day. He was thin. His hands trembled as he hugged Mrs Johnson. He smelled of soap. The skin under his eyes was yellow. I thought: He's been sick. But he won't tell Mrs Johnson that.

I looked into his eyes and wondered what else he wouldn't tell her. Because I'd been down in the dark of ships like that. Not as bad — not near as bad. Captain Phillip had forced us to live, even whipping coves who wouldn't eat their fruit when we stopped to get supplies. But I knew how that dark got to you, how the stink seeped into your soul. Mr Johnson carried some of that darkness now too.

We sat at the table, Milbah on Mrs Johnson's knee. Mr Johnson gave thanks as he always did for what we were to eat, for what God had given us. 'And thank you too, Lord,' he added, 'for the gift of letting us give help to others.'

I stared at him as he finished the prayer. Was that why he'd brought me and Elsie home with him? And helping others made him happy?

I thought how good it felt to dig potatoes for everyone, to know I'd helped look after Mr Johnson's family while he was nursing the sick. Mr Johnson was right.

Sally served us, then sat down as usual. She'd made apple dumplings, so as to give Mr Johnson a treat, made from the first apples from the trees he'd planted, stored in a sack in my lean-to. Mr Johnson pretended to eat. And then he went to bed, though it was still light, and Mrs Johnson followed him.

Things were different after that, not just in our house either. For two and a half years it had been just us, the colonists who'd been on the first ships. We'd landed on a strange land where there were no other white people at all. We'd cut down the trees and built the huts and planted the gardens. We had survived together, even if we didn't like each other much. You knew everyone back then — not their names, but the faces were a bit familiar. Every hut and garden was made by us, and even if the place wasn't as good as it could have been, well, it was all ours.

Now there were strangers everywhere — skinny, sort of twisted strangers, looking as though the light still hurt them after so many months of dark. Right scary, the lot of them. But still no one stole anything from Mr Johnson's gardens. The new convicts, and the ones who'd been here first too, thought Mr Johnson was the best man in the world, the only man who chose to go down into those stinking holds below deck, among the hopeless and the dead.

'Bless you,' one old woman said, grabbing Mr Johnson's hand after Sunday service. 'Bless you for what you did for us.' But she wasn't old, not really, though her hair was white and her back bent. It was just what those wicked, greedy captains had done to her.

There were new soldiers too. They'd made money from those death ships. They'd seen what those captains did and didn't care.

'How can you smile at them?' I asked Mr Johnson one day.

He looked at me with that new darkness in his eyes. 'They are God's children too,' he said.

So is a rat, I thought, as two of the new 'New South Wales Corps' strutted past us, the convicts making way for them like they were Lord Muck and his brother. They didn't even bow their heads politely to Mr Johnson. One of them said something when they were past. The other laughed.

I clenched my fists. I knew they'd said something about Mr Johnson. How could men like that understand a man who cared for the poorest in the world, instead of taking the food from their stomachs to grow rich?

More convicts were assigned to Mr Johnson's gardens now, and to the house too. Some didn't stay long. Mrs Johnson wouldn't have any swearing and it seemed like those were the only words some convicts knew. But the Johnsons gave them chance after chance, teaching them how to speak and even their letters, just like they had for me and Elsie. They were sad every time they had to send any of them away.

But the newcomers didn't understand about Birrung, no matter how much Mrs Johnson and I tried to explain. Us old-timers knew about the Indians, knew they were people like us. We'd met them, talked to them, like kind

Arabanoo or Bennelong, the governor's friends, and Nanberry, who was like Surgeon White's son now, and Birrung too.

'Black savage,' one old lag called her.

'I ain't sitting at no table with a darkie,' said another woman, brought to help Sally with the housework, like she was a queen instead of a pickpocket and Birrung was a rat in the sewers.

'Then you'll do without dinner,' said Sally shortly, just as Elsie gave the new convict a sharp elbow in the ribs. Even Sally loved Birrung just a bit by now.

I wanted to say that Birrung knew everything that mattered, when the stars would say the emus had laid their eggs, how the wattle flowers could tell you if it would be a dry summer. But this woman couldn't even see that those things were important. 'Old sheep face,' I said to her instead, which was the worst insult I could think of that wasn't swearing. 'Baa!'

'Stop it! All of you! Abaroo is part of our family, and God's,' said Mr Johnson sternly.

'Taperabarrbowaryaou,' said Birrung softly. 'But I shall not become white.'

The new convict woman said something I promised Mrs Johnson I'd never say, much less write down. She stomped out and went to work for one of the officers. There were so few women in the colony back then that any who could use a broom and a cooking spoon was sure of a place to live.

Even though they loved Mr Johnson, the new convicts didn't stop swearing, and they couldn't see past Birrung's skin.

That was when Birrung stopped laughing at all, I think, though it was weeks before I realised. She still didn't go down to the harbour. Some lout would yell at her, about her being black and wearing clothes just like she thought she was a white person.

Then one day she was gone.

I'd been working down in one of Mr Johnson's other gardens with Scruggins. I came in for dinner and Birrung wasn't there, and no place was set for her at the table.

For a moment I went cold, thinking she might have got the typhus. But Mrs Johnson just said quietly, 'Abaroo has gone back to her native family.'

'Why?' I asked.

But I knew why. It wasn't just the insults and the yells. There were more white faces than ever now.

Birrung knows, I thought. She knows we will keep coming and keep coming. When we were a few strangers in their land, then the natives could welcome us, stare at us, stay with us like Birrung and learn our ways, think maybe one day we'd learn their people's ways and words too, like I had begun to do.

It wasn't going to happen. I knew it. Now Birrung did too.

Mrs Johnson must have seen my face. She said kindly, 'I think she has gone to get married.'

That hurt me even more. Why didn't she wait for me to grow up, I thought, and marry me? But of course she'd be getting old by the time I could marry anyone.

'I forgot to wash,' I said. I went out to the water trough behind the shed so no one could see me cry.

CHAPTER 13

Presents from Birrung

Birrung visited a few times after that. The first time I'd never have known she'd been there, except for the honeycomb in the bowl on the table, and a great spray of the yellow and purple flowers that clung to the rocks around the harbour, like they lived on air and stone, not soil, and the big fish for dinner.

'A present from Abaroo,' said Mrs Johnson. 'She is looking well.'

It hurt a bit that Birrung came to see Mrs Johnson

and Milbah, and not me. We were living in the Johnsons' new house by then, a good brick one, with proper doors and shutters at every window and even proper beds for every one of us. A proper bed to myself! All Mr Johnson's books came out of the sea chests, smelling of mould. They looked fine on the new bookshelves.

I was away when Birrung and Mr Johnson went as hostages to stay with Bennelong's wife, Barangaroo, while Bennelong went to see Governor Phillip, who had been badly wounded by an Indian, to try to make peace between the colonists and the Indians. If I hadn't been working at the Kissing Point gardens, I could have been a hero like Mr Johnson, risking my life to try to make the colony safe. I could have spent the whole day with Birrung.

I was away working the next time she visited too. Sally said another Indian girl had come with Birrung, and Mrs Johnson said that Elsie had gone for a walk with them. I didn't know whether to be jealous that she was with them, not me, or worried that it was late afternoon, and she wasn't back.

The back door opened. Elsie came in, carrying a big basket woven of grass. Her cheeks were flushed red from the sun, like ripe apples, and her face was full of laughter.

I was jealous of that too.

'Where have you been?' demanded Mrs Johnson, cross because she had been worried too. 'I said a short walk, not the whole day! Is Abaroo with you?'

Elsie shook her head. She put the basket on the kitchen table. She took out hunks of meat, wrapped in grass to keep off the flies.

Sally peered at the meat. 'What is it?'

'Gan,' said Elsie.

I stared, and Sally stared, and so did Mrs Johnson. Had Elsie really said a word? Maybe it had been a baby 'goo' from Milbah, or a sound outside.

'What's gan?' I asked at last. There was something familiar about the word.

But Elsie shrugged. If she'd said a word, she wasn't going to say another one.

Sally fried the steaks. It had been a week since we'd had fresh meat, when Mr White's shooter had shot more wild ducks than they needed at the hospital and he had sent us some. The meat was good, a bit like duck, all fried up with pumpkin and onions and served with boiled cabbage and boiled potatoes, as much as we wanted to eat, and then sliced melon.

I looked at the bones on my plate after we'd finished

116

eating. Like a sheep's backbone, but smaller. And all backbone, no legs.

I remembered Birrung pointing to a curving track in the dirt, then making one finger wiggle like a snake. 'Gan,' she'd said. 'Gan.'

My stomach wiggled too.

I thought: If it came from Birrung, it would be good.

The next time I saw a snake, pretending to be a stick by the track, I thought: Dinner.

It was the summer of 1793 the last time I saw Birrung. It was hot, but the ants were building their castles, the ones Birrung had told me meant that it would rain, so I was up on the hillside above the harbour, cutting bark to roof the new church instead of lugging buckets of water to the vegetables: the rain would do the watering for me soon enough.

It wasn't much of a church, not like the stone ones back in England. But no one was going to order convicts to build one in Australia, even though Mr Johnson said the governor's instructions from England had been clear that one was to be built. Mr Johnson was still preaching in the fields or the old storeroom with the rotting roof when it rained.

I wasn't no builder, just like I hadn't been no farmer, but every man in the colony learned how to put up wattle and daub, unless their brains were too rotted with rum to care if they had a roof at all.

The seagulls yelled and the waves danced. I piled up sheet after sheet of bark.

Someone pointed down the road. They yelled, 'Sails ahoy!'

And there was Birrung.

She wore her white petticoat, her feet bare and dusty, her hair frizzy like all the Indians', not plaited straight like it had mostly been when she lived with us. She walked like she didn't hear the shouts of the men, the whistles.

I grabbed my axe — you couldn't put a tool down in the colony without some lag pinching it — and ran up to her.

I was as tall as she was now.

There was so much to tell her; about the new church and the schools Mrs Johnson had organised, with convict girls she'd taught their letters teaching the little ones in turn, and Mrs Johnson teaching the older ones, and at Sunday school Mr Johnson himself teaching the ones who could read and write and do their sums — like me — about the nations of the world like France and how they'd killed their king, and how to read big words like 'sojourner'.

I stayed close to her till we reached the house, ignoring the shouts from the convicts amazed to see a black girl wearing clothes, and all the rude suggestions. I thought: Maybe Birrung has come back to stay now. Maybe now I'm taller she might even think of marrying me in a few years' time. I had some money saved up by then, and dreams too.

Mrs Johnson came out when she heard the noise. She hugged Birrung and little Milbah hugged her too, and showed her the dolly made of a corncob that Mrs Johnson had dressed in tiny clothes. Mr Johnson was over at Rose Hill, staying overnight after the service, for it was a long weary voyage down the river there and back.

We went inside. Elsie and Sally made maize-flour griddlecakes, sweet with dried currants from our last crop, and a pot of sarsaparilla tea, the flowers dried from the spring before.

When Mrs Johnson gave thanks, so did I, deep in my heart, remembering how hungry I had been and seeing the plenty in front of me, and Birrung sitting at the table again, laughing and eating griddlecakes, just like we'd been before. We all sat and laughed and were happy.

I never saw her again.

CHAPTER 14

I Tell You My Secret

Mr and Mrs Johnson taught me to praise God and to read words. Birrung taught me to see this country as beautiful. She taught me to see the land.

I heard that she came back again a couple of times to see the Johnsons, naked like all the natives, not even wearing her petticoat. Elsie and I weren't there to see it, but why we weren't, and where we'd gone, what happened when the Frenchman came for Elsie, is a story I won't tell you today.

I am an old man now, not a ten-year-old boy, but I can still see Birrung like I did that first day by the mud storehouse, clean and pretty in her blue and white dress. I can hear her voice telling me native words. I've even used some of those words with native people, and they understood them too. I've used all that she taught me, and I reckon Elsie learned things from Birrung I never knew about back then too. I've never shot a black man, like so many of my neighbours, or put out poisoned flour. I've tried to understand and, because of Birrung, known I can't.

So that is my secret. I had a friend a long, long time ago. She was a girl, and she was black.

I loved her.

Now you know my secret too.

AUTHOR'S NOTES

Barney Bean, Elsie and Sally are all fictional, although based on real people. Mr and Mrs Johnson, Mr Dawes, Milbah and Birrung/Abaroo existed. Their lives in this book are based on what is known about them from letters written at the time by Mr Johnson, and diaries and books written by others in the colony.

Mr Richard Johnson was the colony's first clergyman, beloved of the convicts and some of the officers. He was a committed and passionate Christian who saw himself as a missionary to the colony of New South Wales, to the convict and Indigenous populations as well as to the officers. Often described as 'tireless', he was more likely often very tired indeed, building his first house mostly by himself, cultivating the most productive and possibly the largest gardens at the time in the colony, giving Sunday services in the open air or in a crumbling storehouse when it rained, and trekking down to Rose Hill, an outlying settlement, to conduct weekly services there too, while also working as a magistrate, tending the sick in hospital, caring for orphans, and teaching both children and adults to read and write and do sums.

Bennelong went to visit Governor Phillip, who had been badly wounded by an Indigenous man, to negotiate peace in the aftermath of this potentially war-inciting event. Barangaroo, Bennelong's wife, was violently opposed to Bennelong's role as an intermediary between the native people and the colonists, so Richard Johnson and Birrung remained with her as a guarantee that her husband would be returned to her.

Mr Johnson's work was heroic during the hellish months after the arrival of the Second Fleet. Against all advice he insisted on going down into the holds of the ships, among the dead and dying in the filthy darkness, tending them, feeding them from his own supplies and garden. The convicts loved and revered him — even if he couldn't stop them swearing.

By the end of 1789, Mr Johnson had drawn up a

plan for 'dame schools' — small schools supplying a basic education — for the entire colony. He paid for the building of the colony's first church himself, a wattle-and-daub chapel built at what is now the corner of Bligh and Hunter streets. With his wife, Mary, he used the church as a schoolroom during the week and taught over a hundred convicts and their children.

The effort broke his health. Illness left him partially deaf.

So why don't we remember him as a hero?

'History' is created from the letters and documents left to us. Much of what there is to read about the early colony was written by people who resented Mr Johnson because he believed their profiting from starving convicts was morally wrong. Perhaps he made them feel guilty. (People who feel guilty often are angry with the person who makes them feel that way, instead of sorry for their own actions.) Maybe they were also worried that he would hurt their reputations back in England.

Even Elizabeth Macarthur, who left superb letters that vividly portray early colonial life, made it very clear she had no pleasure in the company of Mrs Johnson, a woman who spent her days teaching convicts, not at picnics and in flirtation. The Macarthurs were not just influential in their own time: Elizabeth's letters are one of the chief sources of information about the early colony. Self-sacrifice and dedicated service to the poor and criminal, not to mention physical labour by the 'high-born', do not seem to be choices she valued.

Mr Johnson's work was tolerated by Governor Arthur Phillip, the colony's first governor, who, perhaps reasonably, thought building granaries to keep the colony fed was more important than the church Mr Johnson wanted, and who may have thought, as was common back then, that it was a waste of time teaching convicts how to read, write and do sums. The treatment of Mr Johnson grew far worse when Phillip returned to England, worn out by his work in the colony and the spear wound to his shoulder, which never healed properly. Now the officers of the New South Wales Corps (or 'Rum Corps') took command of the colony. Mr Johnson strongly disapproved of the behaviour of many of these officers, such as Major Grose and Captain Macarthur, Elizabeth's husband, who granted themselves large estates and the right to buy and sell goods and rum. They in turn despised him.

It wasn't until Governor Hunter was appointed that Mr Johnson was repaid for the expenses he incurred building the church. But even then, the Rum Corps encouraged convicts to taunt the chaplain in the street, though not the convicts from the First and Second Fleets, who loved him. The culprits were later arrivals, who had never had anything to do with him apart from compulsory (though not enforced) church services on Sundays. The services possibly brought the convicts little benefit, being hot in summer and cold when the south wind blew, and with Mr Johnson's voice hard to hear over the noise of the wind or the cicadas. They would not even have known the hymns to join in singing.

The church Mr Johnson had built with so much dedication was burned down in 1798, possibly on purpose, even as revenge for his criticism of the corrupt Rum Corps officers. By then the increase in the population of the colony meant that Mr Johnson would have been a stranger to many, and his sacrifices and kindness unknown to them.

In 1800 Mr Johnson and the next governor, Mr King, set up an orphanage. The Johnsons sailed to England in October of that year. It is unclear whether he intended to come back to the colony. By then he was ill, partly from overwork and his struggles against the corruption of the colony, but also because he chose to help tend those who had infectious illnesses. His health seems to have remained frail, and he was offered only temporary, badly paid jobs until 1810, when friends helped get him a better position in London. He died in 1827. Mrs Johnson died in 1831. Milbah had died in 1804, only a few years after their return to England. A son was born two years after Milbah and was still alive after his parents' deaths, but I have been unable to find out anything more about him.

Little is known about Birrung's life after she left the Johnsons and I have been unable to find later references to her in any of the writings from the colony after the Johnsons left. She may possibly have been written about, but under a different version of her name. The last reference I have been able to find is in a letter written in 1795 by Mrs Johnson, saying that Abaroo ... *still visited them.*

Indigenous Words in the Text

These are mostly taken from the records of those years made by Mr Dawes, with further references from the *Macquarie Aboriginal Words: a dictionary of words from Australian Aboriginal and Torres Strait Islander languages* (edited by Nick Thieberger and William McGregor, published 1994) and the notes of the language used in the Sydney region by Jakelin Troy, though all the Indigenous words in the text are ones I have come across in other contexts. However, as with Birrung's name, there are many ways these words have been put into English letters. I hope that 'Birrung' and her people will accept a 'tried to get it as right as I can' instead of 'I am sure that this is accurate'. Dictionaries of the eastern coastal languages are still being put together, from the words people remember, as well as written sources.

Names

BIRRUNG

The Birrung of this book was called Abaroo by the Johnsons and members of the colony, except for Lieutenant Dawes, who recorded the name as Booroong, and as Boo-ron, Birrung and Burrung. As mentioned above, the Cammeraygl and other languages that Birrung may have spoken use some sounds that are different from English, and difficult for English speakers to pronounce or even hear or repeat.

I chose the form Birrung because it is recorded as meaning 'star' in the languages of the Indigenous people of the Sydney region, and the Eora word for 'star' sounded like Booroong or Birrung. Her name might equally have been Burang, meaning 'grass', or Barang, meaning 'stomach'. But as with Nanberry, Bennelong, Colbee and Barangaroo, we may never know what their names really were, either the short form, or the longer names they used more formally and that the colonists were unaware of.

MILBAH

I have been unable to find out what Milbah means, but there are many records of it being used as a girl's name in New South Wales from about 1800 onwards — not commonly, but various different families did choose it for their daughters. The records don't show any other Indigenous name being used in the English community, so perhaps the naming of daughters Milbah was a tribute to the Johnsons' daughter, a gesture of love and thanks for her parents' contributions. In 1816 a baby girl (probably of European, not Indigenous descent) born in the colony was given the name Milbah, according to the birth records, so the name was still being used in the community at that time. Possibly Milbah's parents remembered the kindness of the Johnsons.

Growing Food

Those who have never grown their own food in Sydney or similar climates won't know how fast crops grow, and what abundance can be grown in a small space in a short time. According to the diaries of the early colony, fruit trees were producing fruit within two years. Possibly they were advanced trees when transplanted, but well-watered trees do grow fast. They wouldn't have produced much, but our trees here, in a colder climate, usually produce some fruit the first and second year after transplanting.

Colonists were hungry because they didn't work their gardens, or gather food like oysters, wild spinach, mussels and other shellfish. Oysters were a common food for even the poor in England, so all in the colony would have known they were good to eat, and abundant enough to feed everyone. Those who did, or who had good gardeners, like Governor Phillip, ate well. No one starved even during the time of worst hardship, except for one man who saved his rations to escape to China, and another whose rations were taken as 'rent' to use someone else's pannikin. Nor did Surgeon White record any pellagra from protein deficiency, just scurvy in newly landed colonists after a long voyage. White —

who hated the colony, for the misery he had seen — even described it as the healthiest place on earth. But the colonists were terrified they might starve. They had landed with three years of food supplies. By the time the Second Fleet arrived, their stores were almost gone. Many of the convicts and most of the officers refused to do any hard work, from growing food to gathering oysters. Gentlemen were not supposed to do manual work. Mr Johnson was one of the few in the colony who did. The colony wasn't starving, but they were certainly terrified of starvation, ragged, mostly shoeless, scared they had been forgotten by England and that the colony might even vanish like the Roanoke colony had in North America. Many convicts believed the officers might sail off in the colony's small ship and leave them stranded. All were probably afraid that once the stores ran out, both convicts and officers might steal or commandeer food from those who were growing it, rather than worked, and the colony might degenerate into civil war.

For those who wonder if you really can grow abundant fruit and vegetables, eggs and cheese in two years, even without hoses and a central water system — try it. It will not only give you deep satisfaction — and keep you fed while you begin a career like writing books — but

give you the confidence that, with a few seeds and dead-looking sticks, you can keep yourself and your family fed. It is that security that the early colony lacked.

ELSIE'S SOUP

This is delicious, and very cheap to make. The flavour will change depending on what kind of cheese you use, and what you cook the onions in, and even on what kind of onions you use. Red onions give a sweeter soup, brown ones a stronger onion flavour. Cheap white sliced bread doesn't add much taste at all, but a sourdough white or a French loaf or rye bread or a good multigrain will really make the soup richer. I sometimes use six tablespoons of strongly flavoured, freshly grated parmesan cheese, but gouda is a mild cheese that turns wonderfully stringy in this soup, and tastes good. Feta and cheddar also work, as will probably any cheese that you love best, though again the taste and texture when cooked will vary from cheese to cheese. You can also use stock instead of water, and that changes the flavour too. But every variation I have made has been very good indeed.

Basically this is a soup made from the most simple ingredients, but every one of those ingredients has to be good to make it a great soup, not just an OK one.

30 large onions, peeled and finely chopped (wear
    sunglasses to help stop the juice stinging your eyes)
12 tbsp chicken fat or olive oil or butter
6 thin slices of bread, lightly toasted, about half as thick
    as ordinary sliced bread, fresh or stale
About 12 tbsp finely grated cheese
8 cups water, or chicken, vegetable or beef stock

Place the fat, oil or butter in a pan with the chopped
onions. *Slowly* cook the onions, stirring all the time, till
they almost melt and are a pale gold colour. They must
not be cooked too fast, or they will turn dark brown or
black and be bitter. They also have to be stirred all the
time, or they will catch on the bottom. This slow cooking
changes the flavour of the onions, so they become less
sulphur-like and sweeter and slightly caramelised. They
will take at least twenty minutes to cook, and possibly
much longer. Onions with 'fat' rings take longer to cook
than ones with 'thin' rings. (Once you've cut up an onion,
you'll see what I mean.)

Now place a layer of cooked onions in an oven-
proof pot. Elsie cooked hers on the side of a fire, but it's
easier these days to put the pot in an oven. Add a layer
of toasted bread, scatter on cheese, then alternate layers

of onions, bread and cheese till it is all used up. Finish with a scatter of cheese.

Pour on the stock or water. Place in the oven with no lid on. Cook at 200°C for two hours, or on a lower heat for longer. Serve very hot, scooping up layers of bread, cheese and oniony broth with each serving. It will look a mess but be delicious.

The Secret Histories

Barney Bean and Elsie have secrets, and so does history: there are many little-known events and people in our past. Each of The Secret Histories books will reveal another surprise in our heroes' journeys, as well as something from Australia's early years you may not have read about before.

The Secret Histories Series
Birrung the Secret Friend

Outlands Trilogy
In the Blood • Blood Moon • Flesh and Blood

School for Heroes Series
Lessons for a Werewolf Warrior • Dance of the Deadly Dinosaurs

Wacky Families Series
1. My Dog the Dinosaur • 2. My Mum the Pirate
3. My Dad the Dragon • 4. My Uncle Gus the Garden Gnome
5. My Uncle Wal the Werewolf • 6. My Gran the Gorilla
7. My Auntie Chook the Vampire Chicken • 8. My Pa the Polar Bear

Phredde Series
1. A Phaery Named Phredde
2. Phredde and a Frog Named Bruce
3. Phredde and the Zombie Librarian
4. Phredde and the Temple of Gloom
5. Phredde and the Leopard-Skin Librarian
6. Phredde and the Purple Pyramid
7. Phredde and the Vampire Footy Team
8. Phredde and the Ghostly Underpants

Picture Books
Diary of a Wombat (with Bruce Whatley)
Pete the Sheep (with Bruce Whatley)
Josephine Wants to Dance (with Bruce Whatley)
The Shaggy Gully Times (with Bruce Whatley)
Emily and the Big Bad Bunyip (with Bruce Whatley)
Baby Wombat's Week (with Bruce Whatley)
The Tomorrow Book (with Sue deGennaro)
Queen Victoria's Underpants (with Bruce Whatley)
Christmas Wombat (with Bruce Whatley)
A Day to Remember (with Mark Wilson)
Queen Victoria's Christmas (with Bruce Whatley)
Dinosaurs Love Cheese (with Nina Rycroft)
Wombat Goes to School (with Bruce Whatley)
The Hairy-Nosed Wombats Find a New Home (with Sue deGennaro)
Good Dog Hank (with Nina Rycroft)
The Beach They Called Gallipoli (with Bruce Whatley)

Jackie French is an award-winning writer, wombat negotiator and the Australian Children's Laureate for 2014–2015. She is regarded as one of Australia's most popular children's authors and writes across all genres — from picture books, history, fantasy, ecology and sci-fi to her much loved historical fiction. 'Share a Story' is the primary philosophy behind Jackie's two-year term as Laureate.

You can visit Jackie's website at:
www.jackiefrench.com